Earthrise
and Other Stories

Earthrise
and Other Stories

S.J. Epstein

Sunmarks, an imprint of
Aurora Publishing LLC
135 Ocean Parkway, 17D
Brooklyn, NY 11218
Sunmarks.pub

EARTHRISE AND OTHER STORIES

Identifiers:
ISBN 978-1-938481-46-8 Hardcover
ISBN 978-1-938481-47-5 Trade paperback
ISBN 978-1-938481-48-2 ePub
ISBN 978-1-938481-49-9 Kindle
ISBN 978-1-938481-50-5 Mass-market paperback

Cover image: Collage of "Triple Star Sunset" and "NASA Apollo 8 December 24" both by NASA and in the public domain.

Table of Contents

Introduction

I've always loved the short story—especially in genre fiction. And many classics of science fiction are in the short story form. From "Nightfall" to "The 9 Billion Names of God" to the stories of *The Martian Chronicles*. Even the Hugo-awarded "best series of all time"— the Foundation series—began life as a series of short stories. To a certain extent, in its formative years, the short story formed the core of the science fiction cannon.

I wrote most of these stories between 2011 and 2013; and for the most part, hadn't looked at them since, until recently. At that time, I was writing—at least a little bit—almost every day. Working that way, one builds up a pretty sizeable volume of material.

These stories range from near-space-opera to more intimate, closely-focused ones. And while I do hope you enjoy the entire collection, even if you like just one of these tales, I will have done my job.

.............About the author

—*S.J. Epstein May 27, 2021, Brooklyn*

S. J. Epstein wrote his first short story as a second-grade assignment, and has been passionate about the form ever since, so much so that in college he founded a campus magazine to publish them. He earned an Honorable Mention in the Writers of the Future contest (for the story, "Earthrise," which gives this collection its name). He works as a marketer and copywriter for a global scientific and scholarly publisher. He lives in Brooklyn with his wife, and a growing collection of guitars and other musical instruments and gear.

Cassandra

The lurch almost threw me out of bed. I woke staring down out the porthole in the floor, watching the sun circle by. I sat up, pushing down the dizziness, and reached for my touchphone. I had hitched an almost free ride—I was doing some consulting, even though I'd been downsourced—on the *Cassandra's* space trials. We were three days into it; and there should not have been anything that violent on the standard itinerary.

"Sorry about that, Hans," Captain Matt said, before I'd even spoken. He sounded as annoyed as I felt. "Frankie wanted to push through a few extra maneuvers. I said 'no,' but he over-rode me and went ahead anyway."

"Don't you have authority on your own ship, Captain?" I said, rubbing my eyes.

"This is why I hate space trials," he said. "On space trials, the Head Designer can pull rank."

I rubbed my face. (Were there more wrinkles on it now?) "What exactly did he do?" I asked. A pause. I put on a shirt, and turned on the camera feed.

Matt also rubbed his eyes. "A zig-zag anti-threat move he'd seen in a military manual."

"Huh," I said. "I guess I am out of the loop. No one at the company told me we were planning on taking a civilian cruise liner into combat."

Matt leaned toward the camera, the Eagle on his collar coming in to focus. "Between you and me, I think he wants to pitch selling this propulsion system to the military."

I shrugged. "Fine. But at four in the morning?"

"I know," he said. "Look, I'll tell him you were pissed—maybe that'll get him to back off until later."

You think he'll give a shit what I think? I thought. Instead, I said, "No, look. I'm up already. I was going to get up in another hour anyway. I'll get dressed and go and take a look at the containment systems. See if he's broken anything."

I floated myself into my workstation harness and began running the diagnostics. Frankie had duct-taped a hand-written checklist above my workstation touchscreen. As if I needed it.

First: Secondary magnetic containment on the polywell reactor. Then integrity of the cooling and pressurization system for the entire silane cuperate system. Then a quick check—just to see—of the entire magnetic containment system. Not really my area; but those containment fields— they're what the superconducting pressurized silane cuperate is all about. And I'd feel a little silly and embarrassed if the plasma containment failed, and all I could say about it was, "But the cooling/pressuring system was working!"

I ran the checks, and then, just for kicks, I took a look at the list Frankie wrote up. He'd got it wrong. He'd put checking the magnetic plasma conduits second — right after the primary safety check—and before everything else. Understandable, emotionally—the plasma jets were his main interest. But he'd got the logic wrong—you can't depend on the integrity of the magnetic fields without making sure you've got the right pressure and temperature for the silane compound to superconduct.

"Oh, good—you're up." Frankie floated by, his young bony limbs jutting out of shorts and a T-shirt. "Think the system is up for some joyriding today?"

Am I up for joyriding is the better question, I thought. "What—what do you mean—how much joyriding?" I said.

"Oh, right—forgot to send you the scheme." He tapped at his watch.

The scheme popped up on my monitor. Three days of extra maneuvers, including high acceleration, short breaking, fast turns, off-axis coasting.

Three days.

I couldn't afford three days—I had an appointment with Dean Cohen Yu from Tshingua University. Adding three days to the itinerary would make one day late for that appointment.

Maybe Frankie could see my jaw dropping. He said, "Don't worry, professor—the ship's fast enough—we'll make up the day and get you to your conference with a few hours to spare."

"A few hours?" I said. I had been planning on having a full day. But in any case, a few hours in space travel was cutting it much too close for comfort.

"You'll make it in time," he said. "And you'll get the job, too. I've already posted a reference!"

Crap! I thought. Who invited him to post a reference? That was the problem with professional networking—my interviewers post on my profile that they're talking to me, and everyone in my network can see it. I meant it as a way of making myself seem more competitive—see who's seeing me—I hadn't thought that this kid would take it upon himself to blow my chances with his probably poorly chosen words. What I said was, "I hadn't realized the *Cassandra* was supposed to be a military ship."

"It's not," he said. "But the P15 propulsion system—this could definitely be military grade."

I took a deep breath, closed my eyes, took a few seconds before responding. "Yes, sort of. There's enough thrust developed, in a light enough system. But the infrastructure we've got around it—the cooling system, the containment system—they're not up to military specs."

"Right. No one's saying that the systems here," he waved a hand around, almost sending himself into a spin before he grabbed a handrail, "would be up to the sustained stress of military duty. But a few days of stops and starts? Why not?" When I didn't immediately respond, he added, "You don't see a reason why not? I trust?"

"Honestly?" I said. "There might be some inertia issues—coolant sloshing. We could lose superconductivity."

He tapped at his giant watch. Standard issue for Director-level people. I used to have one. Now, if I wanted one, I'd have to pay for it personally. But not on a consultant's unreliably variable income. "Right," he said. "Yes, that could happen. And we'd lose containment, and the entire polywell/plasma system would shut down. Which would be a sucky pain in the ass... Oh—we'd be stuck for a few hours for re-start—you'd lose more time; I see." He paused. "I'll make you a deal—let's compress some of the maneuvers, cut some of the eval time in between—build in some SNAFU time in case we do need a re-start, and still get you to Mars on time?"

"Frank, look. I do appreciate the suggestion. But that's not the only problem," I said. "With coolant sloshing you could get highly localized temperature shifts."

"Never happen," Frankie said. "Not with this system—it's too compact. The whole thing either stays up, or the whole thing goes down. And I grant, yeah, it's possible we could get a shut-down. But that's why we run tests, right?"

"We also run sims before tests," I said.

"That's a good point," he said, nodding. "We'll do this: We'll go ahead with the maneuvers I've got—I'll compress the schedule; you go run some sims on the first few. I'll check in with Suzanne and with Captain Matt, and we'll get started just before lunch. OK?"

The ship was still close enough in to an EntangleNet beacon that I could get a pretty good video link-up with Cohen Yu back in Tshingua. You could see the influences of the mixed ancestry in his face—almond eyes topped with wavy hair that really wanted to go curly, but couldn't.

"Dr. Loemin," he said. "I do want to say, I am looking forward to meeting you in person."

"And I you, Dean Cohen," I said.

"I have to tell you in advance, however. The search committee looked over your CV."

I knew what would come next. With thirty years in industry; with all my interesting projects and research proprietary, my publishing record was thin. At best. Very few journal articles, and most of those were reviews. None of those articles placed in the top journals (because all of my interesting research was proprietary). And a book—a beginning graduate "supplemental" text that I managed to write without violating corporate intellectual property embargoes. And even that—Maude had had to pull strings to get the permission. (I'd suggested there might be royalties. There were. Not as much as she had hoped.)

I said, "Would it help if I pointed out that my book, *Superconductor*

17

Management for Propulsion, got good reviews as a supplemental text in top journals?"

Cohen opened his mouth, then closed it. His eyes shifted—looking through my CV floating next to our chat window. "Yes, I see," he said. "It might help. Somewhat. No decision has been made. We are, however, a research institution primarily. I would say to you candidly—if I might make a suggestion—credits like those might carry more significance at places weighted more towards teaching."

Yes, they would, I thought. And I had some leads at those places as well—I would be meeting with key people from Tufts and Cornell and Heidelberg, too. But teaching universities tended to have less research money. I chose my next words carefully. "If I may be candid, as well, Dean Cohen. I am also looking in those sorts of places as well. But very few places in the Solar System can match Tshingua's reputation. And almost none can match its reputation in Engineering or Materials Science. And while my publication record may seem thin, I can, when we meet, tell you — "

He cut me off. "Your reputation among your peers does travel, which is why we're able to consider you at all. The Search Committee, however, includes faculty from outside the Materials Science and Engineering departments, and they raised the questions about your CV."

"Yes," I said. "What I was saying was, when we meet on Mars, I can tell you about some of the research I've worked on, that I haven't been allowed to publish."

"I look forward to hearing it," Cohen said. "See you in a few days." He closed the connection.

W e'd already waited for ten minutes when Suzanne came dashing into the conference room.

"Suzanne. Great—we're all here—let's get started," Frankie said. "What's your report?"

Suzanne took her dishevled hair down, ran a hand through it, and put it back into its pony tail. She said, "We've run the re-start drill three times in the last five hours. Can you tell me why you want the impossible? There's no way we can get it under an hour. You want to tell me why you're having us do this now?"

Frankie nodded at her, acknowledging. But not answering. He turned toward me. "Professor Loemin—you ran your sims?"

"I did," I said. "But they're only as good as the information fed into them."

"Did they show anything interesting?" Frankie asked.

I shrugged. They showed what the people who programmed them would expect them to show. Not nearly as meaningful as human experience. "Not so much," I said. "But they wouldn't be likely too, based on the assumptions fed in to them. I don't think they're entirely reliable under the conditions you want."

Frankie nodded at me. "I hear what you are saying, Professor," he said. "And you're right. And that's why I'd asked Dr. van Dam to run those re-start drills."

Right, I thought. Still fixed on the idea of only a full system shut-down. Not the kind of transient failure I worried about. I said, "What drills for failures short of full shut-down?"

"Can't happen," Suzanne said. "System's designed to fail safe."

"Right," I said. "But what if it doesn't?"

"Why wouldn't it?" she asked.

Captain Matt chimed in: "Just as long as we all know where the lifepods are."

Frankie said I wouldn't be needed for the first few maneuvers. In his opinion, anyway. So I decided I would spend the afternoon in the Supreme Class dining room. Likely this would be my only chance at such a thing. So I sat at a granite-plated table in a wood-paneled room, placed over large plate windows built into the floor. The passenger unit spun, making the outer walls into the floor; so if the architects wanted to show passengers anything, it would have to be below their feet. Not unlike old-style glass-bottomed boats, really.

I sat at the table, projection floating in front of me. To the left side, my CV, cover letters, other documents. On the right, the list of posts I'd applied for. So far, Tshingua was the only interview. But I'd heard back from a few of the others, and I was trying to coordinate the people I wanted to corner against their likely symposium schedule at the conference. Was going to be tricky.

I was caught up in a list of abstracts when I heard the crash. I looked up. A hole—perfectly round, evenly scorched, appeared in the forward bulkhead that led to the kitchen. I looked the other way, and saw a smaller hole, same shape, in the rear bulkhead, where the kitchen was. I got up, and walked into the kitchen. The autochef hovered over a mess—a soup pot, ruptured, its contents spilled on the floor. I bent down—two more holes, burned through the pot. And another in the wall.

Plasma jet. Spot containment failure.

What else had it cut through?

I ran back into the dining room and grabbed my tablet off the table, and videoed Frankie. Even before he focused on me, I said, "You've got a spot breach—loose plasma jet."

He gave a smug half-smile. "Not possible. Reactors are still up."

I waved my camera lens at each of the holes in the bulkheads. And then I said, "What else did that jet cut through?"

He looked at me; the smug grin gone. *Affect* gone. "Hold that thought," I said, and videoed Captain Matt.

"Do you know what the hell that was?" Matt said.

"Rogue plasma jet," I said.

I could almost see the train of thought work its way across his mind. First his eyes widened, maybe thinking, "Not possible." Then furrows in the brow. Then the question: "What did it hit?"

I sent him the images I'd just shown Frankie. "I don't know—but this is part of the trajectory."

I saw him turn, probably to pull up a schematic. His jaw dropped. And then I heard his voice over the main PA. "This is the Captain. This is an emergency general evac order. Everybody to the lifepods. Now. Message repeats."

On my way to the lifepods—built into the outer hull of the spinning section—the angular momentum would help push them away—I also checked the schematics. If the jet cut in both directions, it would have cut through the hydrogen tanks, the coolant tanks, and the guidance system.

No guidance system. Coolant and hydrogen leaks. Maybe manageable with a full crew, but without damage control, the hydrogen would get out of control in short order.

I ran into Matt, Suzanne, Frankie, the few other trials crew members at the lifepods at midships—we'd all fit into one. Matt fed us in, closed the hatch, and hit the release. We shot away.

The *Cassandra* shook and shuddered—vapor jets shooting out from the aft fluid tanks. The hull cracked, there was one brief flash by the tanks, which then shot up the length of the keel. And then the pieces of the ship began to drift apart—like pictures of old rockets jettisoning their stages.

Frankie stared out the viewport, mouth open, expression still lacking affect, and now, his face, color. "I'm done," he said. "I'm done. I'm done. I lost a ship. I'm done."

"You're not done," I said. "I'm sure the company has insurance on the ship. You'll be OK. Mostly. And I'm available if you need a recommendation..."

Être Vu

. . . .

In the dream. Facts flooded in unbidden—knowledge retrieved with the slightest of effort. He sat in a damp, dimly lit basement. Two men at the locked door. He knew them—he'd spent the last three weeks with them. They lounged; AK's leaning against the wall. It would be lunch soon—the door would open. He tried to figure out how fast he'd have to be, but, somehow the math—which had never failed him—the math was the one thing that wouldn't come. The door creaked open, he jumped, ran for it, and...

Woke up drenched in sweat. It took a few minutes to realize where he was. He was home—but where was home? When was it? What year, what day? What was he?

He turned to the clock—5:45 AM. He had to be up in an hour to go to the lab. Wait—did he have to be up? Something said that he wasn't going to the lab any more. Which lab? To work on what? A note by the clock: "Take the pill."

He sat up, and took the pill with the water on the nightstand. In a few minutes, some pieces started falling back into place.

He was Francis Powers. Polywell fusion researcher at MIT. Or, actually, he wasn't anymore. The Alzheimer's had seen to that. He was retired, living in his newphew's "in-law" suite in northern New Jersey.

23

He swung his feet over the side of the bed, shuffled to the bathroom, and waited for the physiological changes to make peeing possible. Nearly 80 years old, and (pretty much) everything from the neck down still worked just fine. Mostly. It was just the protein plaques making holes in his cerebral cortex…

He had an experimental drain in his neck that worked with the amyloid—dissolvers (also experimental) he was on. They helped—they'd slowed the disease's progression by several factors. But they were losing their battle with the plaque production. Sometime soon—in a year? Five? Frank would lose his mind. And then he'd lose his life.

The girl—it was the same girl—same green eyes, same dark hair. But here, she was maybe thirty, and she was spectacular. His twenty-year-old body nearly couldn't contain itself at the sight of her.

They lounged on the grass in the Columbia cloister. She held forth on her post doc studies in the polywell reactor. He had trouble understanding it—was it the Alzheimer's? Or was it something else? Facts and concepts chased through his mind like lightning, but the math wouldn't come, so he struggled to follow what she was saying.

Y ou're the famous Dr. Francis Powers?" The young woman took the pile of papers off the crowded office's single guest chair. Her necklace jangled as she moved around. "Can't imagine what you're doing on this part of campus."

"You are Diana Blue?" he asked.

"I am," she said.

"You wrote your thesis on near-death experiences?"

"I did," she said.

"Then I'm in the right place."

"Please have a seat, Professor," she said, slipping into the chair behind the desk. "Look. I've heard about your condition. And while I'm surprised that someone like you would come to see me, I'm afraid that I don't think there's much I can offer to you."

"You're assuming I'm looking for some sort of end-of-life comfort," he said. "In fact, I have some specific questions."

She gestured toward the desk. "OK, then. What kind of questions?"

He took the offered seat. He was blocked in one side by over-stuffed bookcases, and cramped in the back by piles of manuscript printouts. "In your research, have you found accounts of people becoming more open to experiences due to compromised mental capabilities?"

"Sure," she said. "When you're mental guards are down, you can be open to perceptions you'd otherwise reject. I assume you mean, someone in your condition?"

He nodded. "If that condition improves, how do you get it back?"

She shrugged. "Traditionally, that's an easy question to answer. Drugs. Or hypnosis."

He nodded. He did not like the idea of mood-altering substances—he never had. But if that was the way to both get his mind back while staying connected to whatever this other experience had been… "OK. Second question. In your research, have you come across any accounts of—not sure how to describe this—a future life experience?"

"A near-birth experience? Where people have memories of having been conscious prior to birth?"

Frank shook his head. "I mean, like a past-life experience, but from a life that's in the future."

She screwed up her eyebrows. "How would that even be possible? I mean, taking reincarnation simply as an assumption for the sake of argument."

"Aren't you the religion expert? You don't believe in your subject?"

"I have a profound interest," she said. "I have a healthy skepticism."

"Well, as you say, then. Taking reincarnation as an assumption," he said. "In that case… I have good friends studying consciousness, some of them looking at it at least in part as a quantum phenomenon. And time's apparent arrow is an illusion."

"Then you seem to know more about this than I do," she said. I should cite you in my next paper." She laughed.

"I would much rather prefer you didn't," Frank said. "It would only confirm, for many, what many suspect already: The old man has lost it."

Frank sat on a bench on the quad, soaking in the mid-spring sun. He swam in a stream of possibilities. Near the end of one life, could he—in all seriousness—entertain the thought of a new one? And, then, a new life cut short? A little late now, he thought, for doubts. He'd doubled-down on it; this treatment gave him back his mind—for now—at the cost of losing it all sooner. Which wouldn't matter at all, really, if this was right.

"Are you OK?" someone asked.

Frank looked up. Jeff Rubinstein—the medical Principal Investigator running the Alzheimer's trial he was in—hunched over him, round face bleached out by the sun over his shoulder.

"I'm fine, Dr. Rubinstein," Frank said. "Just thinking."

"Aren't you supposed to be getting home soon?"

Frank checked his phone. "I suppose I can flag a cab to Penn Station, rather than taking the 1 Train," he said. "Should get me to the train on time."

"I can call a car, if you want," Rubinstein said, reaching for his phone.

"Thank you, no, I'm fine," Frank said. "You could walk me to Broadway, though." He stood up. Knees a little creaky—but just a little. As they turned to go, Diana Blue walked out of the Philosophy building.

"Professor Powers," she said, catching up to them. "Surprised to still see you here."

"I was just leaving," he said. "Dr. Rubinstein, here, is being so kind as to walk me to Broadway." He paused. "Do you two know each other? Jeff Rubinstein, Neurology; Diana Blue, Philosophy of Religion."

The two young people looked at each other—maybe a beat too long.

"I'm afraid I haven't had the pleasure," Blue said.

"Well," Rubinstein replied, "I spend much of my time up at the Medical School up at 168th Street." He offered his hand, and she shook it. "I am also in the biology and biotech department down here. But I'm only down here occasionally."

"Well, that would be why I wouldn't have seen you wandering around campus before," she said.

They both spoke a little too quickly, and they mirrored each other's motions. Frank could see it, even if neither of them could. "Perhaps you should ask the young lady to coffee," he said to Rubinstein.

"There's a nice place on Broadway," she said.

"It's settled then," Frank said. "We'll flag a cab for me, and then coffee for the two of you."

So your nephew is just going to sit in the anteroom?" Martha said. Martha was Martha Stanwick, U.S. Representative for New Jersey District 5. Frank gently lowered himself into the well-upholstered guest chair.

Martha's district office looked out over Route 4 in Paramus, overlooking the slow traffic and strip malls. Inside, the office glowed with blonde wood and wall-panel TVs, playing simultaneous news feeds. One TV showed a Yankee game in progress.

Martha handed Frank a tablet. "Look at that," she said. "This group—based at Columbia, I think—has gone national. They're making a ruckus about cutting your funding." She caught herself. "I mean—the funding for the polywell project."

He scanned the letter. Signed not by a person, but the Organization for Proper Living (return address: OPL@OPL.org) wrote, in part, "It is no alternative to continue the rape of the Earth only because we emit less carbon. We are the pollution—10 billion humans crowding out the Earth herself; sending species to extinction, bending others to our lame desires. Carbon was only a symptom. The true disease is the market capitalism driven spread of human filth. Fusion is no alternative. The only alternative is to undo what we have done. We must return to nature. We must return to a lower population and a simpler way. Fusion is an illusion."

"Even in my addled state, I know the difference between greenhouse gasses and diamonds and composites," Frank said.

"The fact that they're idiots does not mean they're not effective," she said. "They've got a sizeable following, and many of us in Congress have gotten contacted, urging us to cancel Sandia funding."

"You're not going to do it?"

"Of course not," she said. "But it is making many of us give up other concessions—it's become a bargaining chip for the other side. They've somehow gotten in the door on the Hill. They must be getting money from somewhere."

Diana's voice, at the back of his mind. At one level, he knew he was in her cramped office. But where he thought he was...

She asked, "Where are you?"

He said, "APS April Meeting. In the hall outside the room."

"Explain?"

"American Physical Society April Meeting, where I am giving the first talk on our results after declassification. I am outside the meeting room where I will talk. I am talking to Dorothea." Dorothea, editor, 15 years younger. Had she only wanted his research?

"This is the past?"

"30 years ago."

"OK. I want you to go forward, not back," Diana said. "Go forward, past your death."

"I can't."

"Think of the girl you told me about."

"Dorothea?"

"No. The girl at the university."

The image vanished. Then, he was on the quad, sitting with Joanna. "It is May. I am very anxious about my final papers which are due soon but I have not started. Joanna does not have classes, she is working on her thesis which she will not finish this year."

"Excellent," Diana said. "What are you talking about?"

He was trying to pay attention to the draft he was trying to start on his tablet. Joanna was distracting him. "Did I ever tell you I actually met Frank Powers?" she said.

"I'm trying to get started on my take-home, here," he said. "You're not helping me." He poked at her—and then became conscious of the Secret Service agents watching them from a discrete distance. She was a physics Ph.D. student; she was also the President's daughter. At what point might they think he was a threat, and jump him?

"If you wanted to work, you'd be in the library. You want me to distract you."

"No. I didn't want you to think I was neglecting you," he said. "Which, obviously you do, otherwise you wouldn't be trying to impress me by dropping an unlikely name."

"It's true!" she said. "Not about feeling neglected. About Powers. I was five; Mom was still in Congress, and she was working on the funding for fusion. He was involved."

"Everyone knows he invented fusion," he said. He opened two new windows on his tablet—one to calculate the year Joanna was five, and another to find out when Powers died—he'd have bet she'd have gotten the year wrong and was shocked when she didn't. He'd had aggressive Alzheimer's—The summer of that year, he'd been mostly lucid, but had declined rapidly through the Fall, had been essentially comatose when he and his team got the Nobel, and was dead by Christmas. He was lucky, in a way, that he lived that long—they don't give posthumous Nobels.

"He didn't invent it," she said. "He didn't even invent the polywell. He was just the team leader when they figured out how to get enough energy back to make it make sense. Anyway, that was how I got interested in physics." She paused. "Actually, I don't know if it was that day. Or it was how Mom talked about it. She thought it was going to save the world."

"Didn't it?"

"Not according to Olivia Carr," she said.

He rolled his eyes. Carr held a Chair in the Religion department—his mother's former department—and ran an organization called Eden. Carr had started the group when she was a graduate student, where they advocated for "sustainability." When fusion made sustainability truly possible, they transformed into... something else.

F rank pored over the session transcripts Diana had given him, looking for clues. His speech, slurred during the sessions, had given the
transcription software fits. And even where the language was clear,
it was so fragmented… From the sessions, and from his dreams, he had
only flashes—bits of images—the girl on the hill, the campus in the
sunlight, the dingy basement closet and the automatic weapons. And as
the treatments took hold and his conscious mind became clearer, the
images became fainter.

Read on their own, the transcripts made no sense. With context from the
bits and flashes he had—and the dream diary and notes he'd made—some of
them showed a splinter of a story. But they included also pieces that didn't
fit. Why, for example, did the word "aleph" keep coming up?

He went over and over the latest transcript, eyes fixed on the tablet,
while first the Palisades, and then the George Washington Bridge, streamed
by the limo windows. (Sherri had insisted—if he was going to go for more
treatments, she'd pay for the car to and from 168th Street—even though he
was feeling much more confident.) There it was—every other paragraph, in
the middle of everything else—Aleph. And he didn't even know if the boy
he dreamed himself as was Jewish.

He was still studying the text when Rubinstein came to get him in the waiting room.

"Diana told me you had a long session last week," Rubinstein said.

They've been exchanging notes about me, Frank thought. Which meant, he thought, that maybe what was planted a few weeks back was blooming.

Rubinstein's exam took about an hour, including a painful cerebrospinal fluid sample and much less invasive neurocranial imaging. They talked in Rubinstein's office after that.

"The amyloid drainage in the spinal fluid is up, and we can't see any expansion of the plaques," Rubinstein said. "Your neurological glucose use is also back up—a little above normal levels."

"So that's good," Frank said. "In fact, I feel better."

Rubinstein nodded. "You should. But you know about the downside that we're monitoring? The amyloid drainage is up, which is good. But also the amyloid *production* is up, too. And at some point, your neurons will reach a tolerance with the drug, and then the drain won't be able to keep up with the plaque production."

Frank nodded. "When will that happen?"

Rubinstein looked over at the computer monitor on his desk. He reached over and tapped and dragged at it. He tilted his head. "It's early June now," he said, shrugging slightly. "Looking at the rate, adding in a fudge factor? I can't say for sure—when the neurons will reach tolerance is an individual variable. But I'd guess it would be sometime in mid-Fall. October maybe. But the decline will be pretty quick once it happens."

"What does 'pretty quick' mean?"

Rubinstein grimaced. "Don't make plans for New Year's."

"Well, I'll make plans," Frank said, "I'll just plan to be a silent guest of honor."

Rubinstein said nothing.

"I know this was part of the deal," Frank said. "What I want to know is, what will be the implications for my functioning?"

"It won't be like it was," Rubinstein said. "Once you hit tolerance, with the accelerated amyloid production, the plaques'll grow fast. It won't be gradual—it'll be more like a cliff."

"Are you sure you're not taking our sessions too seriously?" Diana asked.

"I would be surprised that you would be the one of us asking that," Frank said.

"I study the phenomenon of past lives," she said. "I know the phenomenon exists—that is, the phenomenon of the perception. That doesn't mean I know for sure that it actually happens. And in most cases, it in a way doesn't matter. But are you sure you want to spend the little time you have left on this?"

She had a point, but only from her perspective. If you're around 40, and with medical advances people would live to 100, you've got 60 years to go—would you bet them on the chance reincarnation is real? But if you've got a degenerative terminal disease, what are you really betting? A year or so? A few, even, maybe? Of increasing degeneration. If he was wrong, he'd lose a slow decline in favor of a fast demise. But if he was right… "Given the amount of time on the line, it's not such a risk," he said.

"It is your choice," she said. "I just feel bad that I might be helping you waste what time you've got left."

"I understand," he said. "You're not the only one to make that observation." He sat down in the guest chair, and handed her his tablet. "I was wondering, though, if you might have some insight. The word 'Aleph' keeps appearing, without any obvious context."

She took the tablet. "Well. Aleph is the first letter of the Hebrew alphabet. Could be tied in with the spirituality of what you're experiencing."

"I've considered that," he said. "I don't think that's it. I think it's something specific."

"Perhaps try to concentrate on that, today, when you're under?"

On the way from the quad to Broadway, Frank noticed posters, buried amid the others on the bulletin boards, advertising a meeting of the Organization for Proper Living. And that those with questions should contact Olivia Carr.

Frank took out his phone, snapped a picture of the flyer, and sent it to Martha Stanwick.

His phone buzzed a few minutes later—Martha calling on video. He answered the call.

"Thanks for sending that name," she said. "I asked around. You wouldn't believe the dossier that already exists on this girl—Hello sweetie—I'm just on the phone with Professor Powers."

A young girl—maybe about five years old—pushed her way into the camera frame. Round face. Dark hair. Green eyes.

"Sorry about that Frank. This is my daughter, Joanna. Joanna—say hello to Professor Powers—one of the people working to save the world."

"Hello," the girl said. "Are you a superhero or a Jedi Knight?"

"I'm afraid not," he chuckled. "Just a physicist. Just trying to make something so we don't have to burn things and make pollution just to keep the lights on."

"Oh," the girl said. "Well—bye!" and she jumped off Martha's lap and ran off.

"She's taken to doing that—*and* she was born after the pandemic!—jumping in on video calls," Martha said.

"I'm sure that can disarm a lot of hostile conversations," he said. "But what do you know about this Carr person?"

Martha looked away—probably to another screen. She said, "Let's see. She is a doctoral candidate in Literature, she's completed coursework. She started out in high school volunteering for environmental and sustainability causes. But now that we're on the cusp of practical fusion, she's shifted her emphasis. Now she's against *all* technology, full—stop. And that starts, I'm sorry to say, with you."

So Olivia Carr was "aleph." While aiming at Joanna, she'd kill that 20-year-old boy in the dream.

Was this enough to go on? To place *faith* in as unscientific a concept as reincarnation? Enough to risk his life on?

Again, assuming these dreams and visions represented something *real*. He'd feel much more confident if there was some way to find out—something to measure, something to test. Some basis for formulating mathematics on it. But the entire experience was subjective, and the closest he had to anything measurable were the hypnosis session transcripts.

Wouldn't that be something, he thought. If one could devise an experiment to test this? *That* might make the whole thing worthwhile…

"This fusion reactor thing is only going to be an excuse for even more development."

The video playing on Diana's tablet showed a small group, most of them sitting in a circle, in a classroom. One woman—petite, with dark hair and a red streak in it—had gotten up and paced around the room, holding forth. This was the woman who had spoken.

"That's Carr," Diana said.

"She let you in?" Frank asked.

Diana nodded. "Sure. I'm in the kind of department from whence interested parties might come. I didn't draw any suspicion whatsoever. But just watch."

"If they have this kind of technology," Carr said, "for unlimited energy without climate change, there'll be no stopping the rape of the Earth. Imagine every inch of land covered with people and buildings. And even this reactor runs on *something*—and that something is hydrogen—they'll use up the oceans in the thing. It has to be stopped."

"How are you going to stop it?" someone asked. "If there's so little downside, how are you going to get people behind getting it stopped?"

"Good question," Carr said. "We need to get our representatives to stop the research before those bastard engineers get the thing to work. It's funded by the government—we should focus on getting the funding cut."

"How?"

"We need to turn public opinion against the research—we can start here and at other campuses."

Diana touched the screen, to pause the video. "Sounds pretty run-of-the-mill," she said. "A bit of a strange perspective, but nothing violent here."

"Yes, Frank said. "Because they think they have a path of action, and that they have time. What would happen if we took both of those away?"

"You think it's not enough just to have the FBI keep an eye on them?" Martha Stanwick said.

"I think we would have the FBI involved," Frank said. "What I'd have in mind is something of a sting."

"I see that," she said. "I just don't see the point of it."

"Think about it logically," he said. "There are only a few possibilities. Either Carr is harmless, in which case, nothing will happen. Or she could be radicalized and violent, in which case, she would take some sort of action. Either that action will be violent or peaceful. If violent, she'll be caught. If peaceful, the FBI will know for sure to keep an eye out for the future. If nothing, then, probably the FBI would not need to watch so closely."

He got up around 11—or a little bit later—that day, to find a Vmail from mom, waiting for him. He knew she'd have a return trace on it, she'd know if he didn't watch it… He toyed with the idea of letting it run on mute. But checking the clock, he realized he was running late. Instead, he sent a note to his mother: "Mom I c the vdo you sent but running l8 I'll watch it l8ter." Joanna was waiting for him. And she'd been quite specific that he shouldn't be late.

She met him by Miller Theater, by the Power Plaque. She was staring at it intently. "Did I ever tell you that I met Frank Powers?" Joanna Stanwick said. "A few months before he was killed."

"About a hundred times," he said. "'It's why you became a physicist,'" he intoned.

"I'm not one yet," she said.

"Yeah, you are. You're just not a Ph.D. one yet. Just like I'm a writer, just not a published one yet."

She kissed him. "See, you say things like that… Even in the middle of all this—trying to write a thesis while being shadowed by both the Secret Service and obnoxious bloggers… Makes me feel almost normal." She paused. "And then I get something like this." She handed him her tablet, open to an email, which read:

"Joanna. As part of an odd experiment, I have arranged for this email to be delivered to you today, in May of 2051. If the following things are true, please let Professor Diana Blue know.

"You are reading this on the Columbia University campus, probably on the quad, and you might be with a young man—you're a Ph.D. student in physics, he is an undergraduate, probably in literature, or language, or philosophy or something similar. And your mother is President. If any of this is true, then you and I may have established some level of empirical evidence for pre—cognition and possibly reincarnation. Yours, Frank."

"That's bizarre," he said. He felt bit of tightness in his chest.

"Yeah? I thought that too. So I had the Secret Service trace it. It was traced to a 20-year-old server at Sandia that Powers asked in his will not be shut down. It had a script to look for me in the Columbia directory, and send this message on this date. It's real."

"Well, obviously it isn't true," he said. "He got the details wrong. We're not on the quad—we're at the theater. Looking at his memorial."

"He knew that he was dying, but he didn't know some lunatic was going to shoot him at a rally here," she said.

Unless he did *know*, he thought—with a flash of déjà vu…

The "scandal" that spread across social media. The furious reaction from OPL. The videos—bordering on rants—from… From "Aleph"?

A rally in front of a theater. An old man stepping forward. And a flash…

He'd never liked this spot—always felt uncomfortable, anxious, particularly outside the theater. And he'd never really read the plaque before. Everyone knew Powers—father of the practical polywell fusion reactor, savior of the modern world, all-but-Nobel but that he died too soon—just weeks before the announcement—to get it. Even if the rest of his research team had.

"Probably caused a quantum split," Joanna was saying. "That's why he got that wrong." She paused, and stared at the granite plaque. "Francis Powers, Class of 1967. Developer of Modern Fusion Power and Contributor to Treatments for Alzheimer's Disease. Killed outside Miller Theater October 2026."

She took the tablet back from him. "Bizarre—you're right—and nothing to be done about it. It's not as though I can replicate the result." She paused. "But the last thing I don't get—why did he want me to give it to Professor Blue? How did he know she'd be your mother?"

Tranquility

Oskar Petros stared out to where the bright white horizon butted up against the pitch black beneath the full Earthrise. If he squinted, he could almost make out the panel-layers tracking back and forth, turning lunar silica into solar panels. It had been a good business, he thought bitterly.

"Dr. Petros. You cannot put us off like this." Jane Sedgewick, Union Boss, said from behind him. "You wouldn't want a strike to disrupt—"

A strike? "How's that going to help anybody?" he said, turning to face her. She wore a red power blouse and a determined expression.

"It wouldn't," she said. "But these frustrations will find an outlet if left unanswered."

"I know, I know," Oskar said, waving his hand at her. "You know this isn't any easier for me, either."

Her expression softened slightly. "Look, personally, I can sympathize. But this is business, not personal. You have 450 Union employees here you're responsible for."

"The reason I haven't said anything yet is because I am still trying to figure out what to do." He'd recruited most of his workers from Earth; he'd paid for their pricey transport to the Moon, and none of them would be able to afford to get back to Earth on their own.

"Well, you could at least say *that*," she said. "Any statement would help me tamp things down."

Oskar's company, Lunar Energy, harvested solar energy at the lunar surface, captured and packaged it in both chemical and thermal form, and sent it Earthside. There were maybe three or four companies on the moon doing the same thing—LE was the largest. All of them about to be put out of business by the announcement out of China Lake.

After all, why buy energy all the way from the Moon, when the U.S. military had fully scaled up Bussard Polywell Fusion, and was in the process of licensing it out? The reactors were pretty easy to build—it wouldn't take long—not long at all—before they were everywhere.

LE did still have the materials processing side of the business—materials that could best be made at low temperatures in a near-perfect vacuum—other natural resources rare on Earth but plentiful on the moon. But that sideline brought in only ten percent of revenue, and only made sense riding on the infrastructure from the energy business.

"Fine," he said. "I'll talk to the workers tomorrow. We'll set something up during lunch."

"Thank you very much, Dr. Petros. I'm sure it will go fine—we're not unsympathetic." She showed herself out of his office.

She'll run for office someday, Oskar thought. She'd come up as a logistics administrator, and risen to run the union shop at LE. And what the union did at LE drove what the union did at the other companies.

He sank into his desk chair, feeling heavy even in the light lunar gravity. He touched the screen. "Call Rex," he said. He was going to need to talk to the bank.

Rex appeared on the screen, straightening the real silk tie under his real wool suit. "Oskar. Nice to see you. How's the family?"

"How's the family?" Oskar said. "Do you really want to know? I'll tell you. Lindie still hasn't realized what's happening—she's still young enough to be excited by the fusion. Kayla, on the other hand… Well, she's probably more anxious than I am."

"Well, I can understand that," Rex said. "I'm affected by this too, you know."

Really? Oskar thought. He didn't think anything could hurt the banks. "I think you know why I'm calling," he said.

Rex nodded. "Yes. Not hard to anticipate, so I've already been looking some things over. Not just for you, but for the others—really almost everybody on the Moon. You're better off than most—you had a lot less debt than some others."

"I thought I had no debt."

"Well, not really," Rex said, "just your revolving business credit—that you use to buy supplies and shipping and stuff."

"So I can use the whole liquidation."

"Yeah," Rex said, bobbing his head.

Oskar opened his balance sheet on another monitor. All the assets spelled out—the office, the plant, all the equipment, all the current supply stock; plus banked energy and finished panels and special materials. Balanced against the cost of shipping the products back to Earth.

"But," Rex said. "You have to consider that, even as we sit here talking, the value of your physical plant is plummeting. The Moon, ironically, is becoming radioactive, figuratively speaking." He looked away from the camera. "I've got your inventory and balance sheet here—I'll update it with the current prices, and email it over to you. Should I assume you're going to want to proceed with the liquidation?"

Oskar nodded non-committaly. "Probably," he said. Not that he saw any alternative.

"I'd suggest you not sit around," Rex said. "The one cost that's going up is Earth-bound passage. The longer you wait, the more it'll cost to move back Earthside."

"Yeah, I'll keep that in mind," Oskar said, and he shut the connection.

Oskar had to get outside—he had to clear his head. He got in his looneysuit and went for a walk out by the old Tranquility Base.

Nothing but a waist-high wire fence kept anyone with a functional moonsuit from violating the landing site. Beyond the fence, the *Eagle's* base with the Nixon plaque, the old wire-stiffened U.S. flag, the footprints. Either the Lunar Territorial Government counted on the idea that no one with a moonsuit would trespass, or they simply didn't care. At least, not enough to spend any money on it, even though it was only 100 meters from Tranquility City's outer wall. Hardly anybody living on the Moon came out here. And with the cost of lunar travel so high, no one came from Earth.

I could break my helmet seal, Oskar thought, *and pass into history—become a permanent part of the site.* He could freeze himself there—an ersatz astronaut statue.

Well, probably, they'd cart his body away. But they'd probably at least lay a plaque. Maybe a vacuum-frozen flower bouquet to mark the spot, not too far from the one from 98 years before. He could macabrely toy with the image, but contemplating actual suicide? Unthinkable.

All would soon be lost. Thirty years before, he'd sold his stake in their family's carbon business to his older cousin Simon, and used the cash to start Lunar Energy. He couldn't stomach the thought of going back to the carbon business—back to Pennsylvania to turn coal dust into graphene, nanotubes, and vapor-deposition diamonds. He'd have to get used to it, he thought.

He turned to go back home. Home, at least, for a little while longer. He still had to figure out how he was going to come up with the cash to get his employees back to Earth. He owed them that much, at least.

But when he got back to the airlock, he found it on lock-down—it wouldn't open.

"Tranquility egress control, this is Petros. Requesting re-entry."

"Petros, Tranquility. Negative. We've got a walker in the airlock."

Walker! Oskar thought. Someone attempting suicide by going out the airlock without a suit. Not easy to do, given the airlock surveillance and the fact that the computer wouldn't let the lock open if it saw someone without a suit.

He pressed his helmet against the airlock window. Hunched in the corner, a figure in most of a suit. The helmet was off, on the floor next to the figure's feet—bare feet.

Clever, that, Oskar thought. Figuring that the cameras wouldn't look down that low. Go into the airlock with a complete suit, helmet and all. But without boots.

"I see him, Tranquility," Oskar said. "Who is it?"

"Rih Shun Lih. Do you know him?"

Rex, Oskar thought. That was Rex's "real" name.

"Yes, I know him well," Oskar said. He peered through the window again. Rex slumped away, facing the corner. The inner lock door sealed—probably digitally jammed by Rex, the outer lock door jammed by Tranquility Control. Impasse. "We both came up to the Moon on the same ship—he's been a friend since." Not entirely true—Rex emigrated to the Moon 15 years after Oskar. But if he could help save a life with a white lie? "Any chance you'd patch me through?"

"The cops are on their way, Petros," Control said. "They'll get him out."

"Could it hurt?" Oskar said. "You've got the outer door sealed, right?"

Pause. Some whispering off the line. "OK, we'll pipe you through. But the cops will be monitoring, so they'll cut you off if they think you're headed in the wrong direction."

"Understood, Control. Rex—it's me—it's Oskar. You OK?"

"Do I look OK, Oskar?" Rex said. "And where are you?"

"I'm outside. Waiting to get in."

Rex stood up, and peered out the airlock door. "Well, then. Open the door and come on in!"

"Can't. Lock's occupied."

"The person there wouldn't mind if you opened it up," Rex said.

"Then I would be guilty of murder," Oskar said.

A pause. "Didn't think of that," Rex said. Then he fell silent.

"What are you doing in there, anyway?" Oskar said. "Why this, now?"

"I can't go back to Guangzhou," he said. "I... I can't. I love living on the Moon. But I can't go back to China. And especially not as a failure. And I thought, this way, I could be part of something important on the Moon forever."

"How are you a failure, Rex?" Oskar said. "I hadn't even heard that the branch was closed."

"Not yet," Rex said. "But that's just a formality. With cheap fusion on Earth, no industry for the Moon, there won't be any need for any banks up here anymore."

"Suppose you're right about that," Oskar said. "How is that your fault? How is it your fault—how did you fail—because people you had no control over made something new?"

"Maybe it works that way in the West," Rex said. "But in my family... My father laughed at me when I went into banking. And he laughed harder when I said I was going to the Moon. And then to go back, like this?"

Oskar nodded. He'd felt some of the same things. How could he go back, hat in hand, to Simon? But he'd find a way. He'd find *something*. He could not imagine actually killing himself. But he could imagine, in practical terms, anyway, better ways of doing it than trying to walk out the airlock without boots. You'd never get very far—your feet would freeze off... He said to Rex, "You know, if you want to talk about failure... This idea of yours, trying to walk barefoot in the lunar sand? Wouldn't work. You'd step outside and your feet would freeze off—you'd end up face-down in the dirt. And, likely as not, your suit would seal up at the ankles. So you'd still be alive. Just without feet."

Silence from Rex. Then: "I thought if I didn't purge the air first, the pressure would push me most of the way to the *Eagle*."

Oskar—trained as a materials scientist—ran some numbers in his head. "Probably about a third of the way," he said. "So you'd be face-down, maybe 50 meters from the door. Talk about lack of dignity!"

"I hadn't thought about it that way," Rex said.

"Well, if you hadn't thought it all the way through, then maybe you don't really want to be dead."

"No, I guess I don't," Rex said. "I just don't see any way out."

"We'll find something," Oskar said. "Now just release the inner lock, and let the cops come get you."

"Yeah. I guess," Rex said. "You know, it's a shame, though, too. After us, almost no one will see Tranquility or the *Eagle* again."

Yes, Oskar thought. A real shame. A real piece of human history that almost no one would see, once the colony was packed up and shipped back Earthside. Even as fusion made energy cheap—even now that BoeingBus would start making micro-fusion propulsion engines—no one would be coming to the Moon to see this.

Unless… He started running some other calculations in his head. Could it work, commercially? Moon tourism had never taken off before, but with the energy equation changing…

"Hey, Rex?" Oskar said. "By the way, once we get settled inside? I'd like to see if we can run some numbers on something new."

Two years later, June, 2069. Oskar stood to one side, watching Jane Sedgewick—now Mayor—give a short speech while wielding an enormous pair of scissors. Workers had strung a ribbon across the corridor leading the 150 meters from the old city wall to the new Tranquility Base Dome Oskar had built.

"We have Dr. Petros to thank for this new lease on Moon life," Sedgewick said. "He sold nearly everything he had—gave up what had been a successful energy harvesting business—to finance and build this dome—and others like it at other landing and historic sites. To say nothing of getting other Lunar Leaders to invest in expanding the space port! Tranquility Base Dome opens to the off-world public next week—and already, the hotels are booked solid for the next year!"

The next year—the centennial year, July to July, 2069-2070, of course. Oskar looked out into the crowd, and caught Kayla's eye. She smiled back at him. He turned to Rex, standing next to him on the dais. "Couldn't have done it without you," he whispered.

"Let's just see if the tourists keep coming, after the centennial," Rex whispered back.

"They will," Oskar said, "they will."

45

Earthrise

On a tour—on a normal tour—Richard would try to go on a daily run; outside, on real roads, in the real air. It was how he'd get a sense of a city, even when the tour consumed the day, even with the smooth-headed Rengle guards on the street corners. He'd run, with just music in his ears, and the rhythm of his feet, through the downtown of whichever city they were in. It was his escape valve; his release from a tour's dull gray ennui.

But this particular tour—20 light years from Earth, on the Occupier's Planet—

The Rengle guards kept the band confined in the land yacht; and already the tension hung in the air like dry ice smoke. Imagine what this would be like, for years at a time, Richard thought. What bands like the Beatles had endured. The surprise wasn't that the Beatles had broken up; it was that they stuck it out as long as they had.

That was without even mentioning Quentin, hired to fill in for Steve, still in a Rengle holding pen back on Earth. Not only did Quentin possess typical lead guitarist pathologies; he was also 20 years younger than the rest of them; 20 years more impulsive; 20 years less wise. But he'd had the idea to add a few new songs to their setlist, mid-tour; which required rehearsal space. The Rengle—to everyone's surprise—had acquiesced, and so the caravan pulled into an empty warehouse somewhere along some backwoods Rengle highway.

Richard stood on the top step of the cruiser watching the crew, black t-shirts contrasting with bald pale-gray skin. The one in the "Road Manager" t-shirt set up the mixing board and monitor system; and other Rengle he'd never met set up his drums, Keith's keyboard rig, Quentin's pedal board and amp cabs. As they set up the rigs, they tested them out by playing riffs and bits of songs.

He knocked on the hatch. "Guys. Check this out." Keith and David came down the steps, and stood next to Richard. Quentin hung back, staying just inside the doorway.

"They're pretty quick at this," Keith remarked. "Don't remember our own crew being this quick at setting up our rigs."

"Must be that big long thumb," David said.

"Maybe fear of what happens if they're not efficient," Keith said.

"Yeah—there's that," David replied.

"But check this out—three fingers, and they still find a way to play a six-string guitar," Richard said.

"All right—cool it," Keith said, holding up a hand.

The crew finished setting up the rig, and then launched into a version of an Earthrise song, "Standing Up."

"They're pretty good," David said to Keith.

"Surprised they'd even ever heard that song," Keith said. "Let alone play it."

"The censors never let us release the song—we only play it live," David said. "How'd they even know it?"

Good question, Richard thought. Even their own fans—their human fans—on Earth wouldn't know the song unless they'd been to an Earthrise concert. Never been released. Never even uploaded to the Net, as far as anyone knew, because doing so wouldn't just endanger the band but also anyone who'd put it out there.

They spent four hours on the new songs. Keith, David, and Richard—over Quentin's objections—invited the crew to act as an "audience," even as they worked out kinks and worked through the older songs. Behind his kit at the back, Richard had a pretty good sense of everything happening on stage in front of him. Even if he (mostly) only saw his bandmates' rears. Going through the songs—even as the rest of them worked off rust and forgotten transitions, Richard noticed that the kid—Quentin—as annoying as he was—could play. It wasn't just that he'd prepared for every note on the set list they sent him when they were preparing for this trip. He knew everything in the added songs. And what he didn't know—you could hardly tell because he'd come up with something you'd thought ought to be there. Richard shook his head. It wasn't fair—Richard had to work, focus on every note, every beat, every subdivision of rhythmic time. But this kid—who seemed to know little else—this kid could just *play*.

When they finished, the crew instantly broke the rig down and packed it up. Richard tried to get out of the way as fast as he could, and found himself next to Quentin, separated from Keith and David. Quentin held his Les Paul by the neck. Stevie used Fenders, mostly; the heavier guitar was one of the major shifts in the band's sound.

"Not a bad way to spend a few hours," Quentin said. "If it wasn't for all the grey-baldies."

"Whatever," Richard said. He walked away from Quentin, and back toward where the crew was heading back to the crew yacht. 15 of them in the same sized space the 4 band members shared. Can't be pleasant, Richard thought. He said to Gasat: "You guys in the crew do a fantastic job," he said. "Think you'd mind joining us for a drink?"

They sat in a bunch on folding chairs—3 band members and 15 Rengle, drinking bad beer and decent scotch. Scuffed concrete painted gray on the floor, walls and vaulted ceiling made of some material Richard couldn't identify. The warehouse so big—like those old NASA hangars—it almost felt like outside, complete with a damp evening breeze. But it wasn't outside; even as he'd hoped to see at least a little of the place—outside the arenas and the grey-green blur outside the (tinted-over) cruiser windows.

"So, what I want to know," Richard began, "is, why—what is it that you've got these city centers, and then huts, and then fields, all in the same order, all over, everywhere we pass?"

"The Masters built the cities," Gasat said. "And they built the farms. And they built everything in that order. All over the world. The huts, we used to live in before. Some people still do."

"So—I don't understand—didn't your people build all this?" Richard said. Aliens show up in orbit with big warships, tell you they have FTL travel and energy weapons, and take over your governments. And then they didn't even invent the stuff? "What are these 'masters'?"

The Rengle looked at each other, perplexed. "You don't know?" Gasat asked. "What do they teach you on Earth about history?"

"Rengle history? Nothing."

"Maybe 400 years ago. The Masters came. They built all this—all these things. The cities, the ships, the machines. Mabye 30 years ago, they left."

"And they left all the tech behind?" David asked.

Gasat nodded.

"Even most of us speak their language," another one said. "A few keep the old language."

"You mean, when you're not speaking English," Keith commented.

Gasat nodded.

"So, these 'masters' conquered you, built this technology, then suddenly left," Richard said. "What happened when they left?"

One of the older Rengle spoke up, in their own language. Gasat translated: "Most of us here are too young to remember. But Rikand was a kid when it happened. He says that, in a few months, they all packed up, they were all gone. No one knew why. They left almost everything behind. And since we'd served them, they'd trained a lot of people in how to work the machines. There had been a resistance, but all the leaders who worked with the Masters left with them. So only SanGarer and the other Resistance leaders were left to lead us."

"So then why did you invade Earth?" David asked.

More murmurs among the Rengle. Then one of them said, "SanGarer and the others found out about you in the Master's records. We sent the army to protect you. Because SanGarer knew that the Masters would be coming to enslave you, too."

"If the idea was mutual protection, then why are we under occupation?" Richard said.

Gasat translated: "We have heard about the terrorists that do terrible things. Blow up transport stations and banks and public places. Kill people. Even some here have started doing that, too. We were told that the army is used to stop the violence."

"Chicken and egg," David said.

To the Rengles' confused expressions, Richard explained, "Earth animal—female lays something called an egg; the new chicken is born from it. But how do you get the first egg, for the first chicken, without there being a chicken first? Here, the question is: Would there be a Subway—I mean the resistance—without the occupation?"

"We are told: You are friends; you are not occupied," Gasat said.

Richard replied, "I can tell you that we live under occupation. It's like what those Masters did to you." He rubbed his face. "You hear our songs—you even did one before, when you sound-checked—about it. We can't even release that one on Earth because it could get us arrested."

"Is there labor conscription?" one of the others asked.

"No," Richard said.

"Yes," Quentin said.

Richard turned to look. Quentin stood at the top of the stairs by the hatch.

"Computer engineers were rounded up and brought here," Quentin said. "My dad was one of them. They came here and wired the place. Built all the computers and networks on the planet."

"I had no idea," Richard said. Surprised that this was news to these Rengle, he wondered how the average Rengle-in-the-street would feel about being to Earth what their Masters had been to them.

The party broke up shortly after that, after they'd drained most of the scotch bottles. Keith, David, and Richard retired to the yacht, and the Rengle roadies packed up the folding chairs.

Richard opened his tablet. Steve had sent an email and another video clip—this one of the well-known writer Sharon Eisen giving a reading in a small café, possibly somewhere in the capital. Didn't know they'd dragged her out here too, Richard thought.

"So, that's what they let me put in my books on Earth," she said to a crowd of Rengle. "Now, let's talk more frankly. Who's got questions?" A raucous shot went up from the crowd.

He paused the clip and read the rest of the email. Steve wrote, "I actually got this clip from one of the guards—it's not circulating on Earth. But I've made 'friends' with some of the guards, and they've been showing me this stuff that they're getting from back home. Huge interest in human writers."

"Think they're wasting their time with writers," Richard wrote back.

Later, Steve wrote back, "You sure about that? The right word in the right ear—or maybe the right paragraph in front of the right eyes—can start something. Cronkite on Vietnam. Gorbachev and Yeltsin. If that wasn't the case, why would authoritarians even bother at all with censorship? Yet our vichy 'government' does it all the time. They think your words could cause them trouble, right?"

O n the throne behind the drum kit, behind the footlights, Richard could hear the audience in his monitor mix, but couldn't
see anything past the third row—all washed out by the stage
lights. Except the lighters when they did the ballad—the one ballad he'd written after that bad break-up with Rebecca. He hated that
song—no, he hated *doing* it—it just didn't really fit with the rest of the
set. But it had been one of their few mainstream hits, and they always
had to have it in the set. They were half-way through—at the first chorus—of "American Heart" when Richard thought he heard something
coming from back stage. They were ramping up and through the chorus, Richard adding harmony from behind the drum kit: "Defeat at the
start/ Was just the first part/ The Empire thought it'd won/ But in eight
years, they'd run/ Beaten by American heart"

He thought he heard something crash—loud enough to come through
the monitor mix—perhaps the pyrotechnics malfunctioning? David and
Quentin both came toward the back of the stage—they'd heard it too. The

three of them looked at each other. David shrugged. Richard nodded at them both, as if to say, "Rule 1: Keep going." Through the rest of the song, and the rest of the set.

Later, after the encore, by the back stage door, Richard saw it all: There had been an explosion. And shots fired. There'd been a bomb planted by the stadium door. While organizing damage control, Gasat had been shot by the Rengle security forces, and taken to the hospital. And on the ground, not even covered, was the tour's chief of security, dead.

T he Rengle government news isn't saying anything about last night," David said, flicking through his tablet.

"They're suppressing it," Quentin said. "About the pro-Earth protests that were apparently happening at the same time. At least they're consistent."

"Word is getting out," Richard said. "I wonder if there are protests like this elsewhere, too. Funny thing is, after trying to suppress it, probably more people are going to see our final show than would have before."

"Yeah—about that," Quentin said. "I, uh, have a message from some people Richie used to know. That I'm supposed to give during the final show."

"Which people, exactly?" Richard said. In college—before he'd met Steve, David, and Keith—Richard had flirted with The Subway—the underground resistance. He'd left when the band took off.

"Oh, I know which people," Keith said, wiping his glasses on his shirt. "Bad elements Richie used to run around with. Sandhogs. TWU. Those sorts," he said, voice clipped, lips tight.

"Dump the euphemisms, Keith," David said. "You're in The Subway, aren't you?" he said to Quentin. "Don't Fucking deny it."

"No shit," Keith said. "Now it all fucking adds up."

David had taken Quentin's acoustic guitar, and had started strumming it.

"I jumped at the chance even just to play for you guys," Quentin said. "I said I was psyched to play with you guys—that's true. But also once this came up, we saw a chance to really let the gray-skins have it. Actually I was supposed to pick a good target, and then stay out of the way, but they kept us locked up…"

"So that explains the hollowed-out amp cab? The one that's too light?" Richard said.

"You spotted that?" Quentin said, nodding. He took the guitar from David, quickly tuned it by ear, and handed it back to him. "There's stuff built into it—in the cab walls. Not so much stuff; I was supposed to pick something I could do with only a little. But security was so tight, I could never get to it, or get away to do anything, anyway. So the only shot left was to use the final show."

"No way. Not acceptable," Keith said. "Earthrise doesn't do violence."

"Are you kidding?" Quentin asked. "You guys—Richie especially—were never fans of the occupation. We—I—thought I could get you guys on board."

"What do you think this would accomplish?" Richard said. "Other than getting us all arrested—and who knows what would happen to Steve—who's still in jail on Earth. What do you think *would* happen, after your amp cab went boom?"

"I wasn't going to blow up the stage," Quentin said. "I was to make a package and put it somewhere."

"Somewhere—you mean, like backstage? *While we're playing?*" Keith said.

Quentin shrugged. "It wasn't supposed to go down this way. I was supposed to blow up a hotel lobby or something. But as that wasn't an option anymore, I had to hit whatever I could. This was the last shot."

"Attacking our own crew," Richard said.

"We can't just sit back and take it!" Quentin said. "They over-run our home, force people to come here—and then they have the nerve to pretend like we're the oppressors? I don't fucking think so."

Richard threw his tablet across the trailer. "You still don't fucking get it, do you? Because of you, someone got killed *protecting us*. Gasat—who *some of us* had grown to like—has a bullet in him. And this is supposed to *help?* And if they figure out that the bomb came from you in the first place. What do we get—arrested? To die here?"

"Rebecca was right," Quentin said. "You've got no balls. You write songs about standing up for freedom. But when the chance comes to really do something about it, you bail."

Richard shook his head. "If I thought spending the rest of my life in a cell here—or getting killed here—would make a damn bit of difference to Earth, I'd do it. But it won't."

"Sure it will! Make the occupation too damn expensive, and force them to leave," Quentin said. "Every resistance is built on that."

"Only when there was a credible movement against that occupation back home," Richard said. "Or else you don't get Britain leaving the U.S. in 1789 or India after Gandhi; you get Rome crushing—well crushing everyone who stood up to them. And there's no such movement here."

"Although apparently—there is," Quentin said.

"And how was a bomb supposed to help with that?" Richard said.

For a change, Quentin said nothing. *Got him on* that *one,* Richard thought.

David was still strumming away, almost oblivious to the shouting. He could do that sometimes, but he heard everything. This time, he said, "Kind of occurs to me that most of the gray-skins still don't know what goes on on Earth. They think their army is protecting us."

"Got a point there, Davie?" Keith said.

"Yeah," David said. "What would happen if they did find out? On a grand scale? That they're acting like those Masters they're so afraid of. Maybe that's what we could do."

"If they haven't gotten it from all the songs of ours that they claim to love…" Keith trailed off.

"Yeah, but, they take those as being about them, not about us," David said. "What if we did a song, about this, for them?"

"So write a song about them as occupiers?" Richard said.

"Yeah. Write and play for them," David said. "Like all our songs about this are about resistance. You say they see themselves in it—themselves and their Masters. But what if we did it so it was about how they treat us—and about then how the Masters treated them."

"That would be an interesting idea," Richard said, rubbing his chin. The lyric would have to both accuse and sympathize at the same time. As he thought about it, images and words began to click together. Helped along by David's chord progression.

The view from the throne: Quentin to the left, David in front and a little to the right, Keith and his rig further to stage right. Richard glanced to his left, where that bogus amp cab would have been. Beyond that, the light curtain thrown up by the footlights, thrown down by the suspended lights, thrown at them by the spotlights. Through the luminous haze, he could almost make out the crowd, but not quite. He'd asked to have crowd noise in his monitor mix, and for the first several shows, Gasat hadn't wanted to do it.

He could have gotten caught up in it—in the emotion rolling through the stadium—maybe across the planet. The chorus David wrote was a classic. And there was the euphoria of throwing caution to the wind. And that the Rengle were responding to it. Was this what they meant by living in the moment? That maybe it was all worth it, in the here and now, even if it failed, even if they all ended up dead, even if…

David's vocals were spot-on; sweet in some spots, raw in others. Quentin seemed to throw himself into his parts more than before; he seemed for the first time to enjoy the feedback from the Rengle audience. They'd built the chorus around a simple major chord harmony, "Things that happen faster/ You become the Masters." For graphics, they ran pictures—taken from their own cameras—of the occupation. And they ran the lyrics in English; and in

57

Rengle translation. They got to the first chorus, with the words flashing on monitors throughout arena—throughout the planet, really—and the crowd's roar became so loud it almost overwhelmed Richard's monitor mix.

At the end of the song, Quentin grabbed David's mic off the stand. "You like that?" he shouted in the mic. "You guys like that?"

David wandered back toward the drum kit, shrugging. They both looked at Keith, still over by his keyboard rig. Keith spoke into his mic, "We've got another song we'd like to do for you." They had six more songs left in the set.

After the last song, they jogged off stage, back to the tuning room. Gasat—still bandaged from the terror attack—met them there.

"You should hear this," he said, turning on an audio feed from the audience.

The crowd chanted, "Free Earth!"

But Gasat looked worried.

"What is it?" Richard said to him.

"The police are outside," he said. "The bad kind of police. The crew is worried."

Richard guessed that the Rengle government had decided not to raid the concert—too much bad publicity. "Guys, I think we have a shot at doing something here," he said. He sat on a counter with his tablet on his knee, writing out new lyrics. "You want Earth free/ You can't want it more than we/ Stand with us/ Stand up with us/ Everyone their own masters." He showed it to David, who nodded. He gave the tablet to Gasat, "Can you get this to David's lyrics monitor?"

"Yes," he said, "I got it." And he ran off without the tablet.

Richard showed the lyrics to Quentin and Keith.

"See you up there," Quentin said, and he ran off. A second later, they heard on the audience feed where Quentin went. He said, "Hello Rengalia! You like the new song? Well, there was a guy on Earth, wrote some words we all like. He said that we were all—all intelligent life—was created equal, endowed with unalienable rights, these being life, liberty, and the pursuit of happiness. And that's what we're all about. You want to hear more?"

The crowd kept shouting.

"I think that's our cue," David said.

"Yeah," Richard said, "let's go."

The three of them ran back on to stage, and the band went back in to the new song, with the new lyrics in outro chorus. The crowd got even wilder, and Richard tried to imagine—if the live feed was still going out—the reaction of those watching elsewhere.

They played another 15 minutes, and then, exhausted, filed off the stage, and right into a waiting troop of military police.

"I'd think they'd move us to a detention center, at least," Richard said, rubbing his eyes. His tab was lit up with messages. One from Steve, just a subject line: "What did you do??" Followed by interview requests forwarded from the band's management office. Probably better to keep a low profile for a while, Richard thought.

"Dude, check this out," Quentin said, staring at his own tablet. "The waves from this made it all the way back to Earth."

"How do you get email from your associates without getting tracked?" Richard said.

"My dad was an Internet engineer?" he said. Richard looked over his shoulder at his tab. The people in the Subway didn't know what to make of it. The people in the blogs… Well, they might know what to make of it, but wrote in rather circumspect terms. One vlogger—whom Richard suspected wasn't human—went so far as to blame Earthrise for kicking off the Rengle Spring.

A troop of Rengle police disrupted the euphoria. "Good morning," the senior officer said. "You may call me Jones. You are Richard Smith, David Cohen, Keith Wells, and Quentin Stone."

"Lawyer," David said.

"I second that," Keith added.

"You are not at this time being detained. Arresting you at this time would only make things worse," the Rengle said. "I am here to try to calm this problem. Which means getting you on a ship back to Earth as quietly as possible."

"What happens when we get back to Earth?" Richard said.

"Nothing," Jones said. "Also, Steve Woods has been released. You have expressed an opinion; you've done nothing else. But you will go. Now. Your items will be sent separately. You will go. Now."

As they drove away from the arena (in the center of the city), Richard saw crowds of Rengle—sometimes large crowds, in some places just a few—lining the roads. Carrying signs saying things like "Let Earth Rise" and "We're Not Masters," and chanting. "Look at that," he said to the other three.

Quentin leaned over, and looked out the window. "Would not have thunk it if I hadn't seen it," he said.

"Wouldn't have gotten this with a bomb," Richard said.

"Yeah. No. You're probably right," Quentin said. "It wasn't just us, though. I'm hearing that the other guys they brought over pulled the same kinds of things. We put it over the top, though."

"Those Rengle are working for us now," Richard said. He snapped a few pictures with his tablet, and wrote an email to Steve, with the subject line of "Orange Revolution." It might take weeks, or years, he wrote, depending on the reaction. They could delay it; the Rengle and the entrenched human collaborators; but they couldn't stop it. Eventually, the Rengle would leave.

And Earth would rise.

...............Entanglement

Jeff stood in the cavern of the emptied building, surrounded by nothing but the vast concrete floor, concrete pillars holding up the ceiling, and gloom. The chill he felt, he was sure, was his imagination. He hadn't felt it the last time he'd been in this building—at least, not before hearing that eerie voice…

He watched as his friend Rachel hooked up the gear the two of them had just lugged up from Wadsworth Street. They'd made four trips from her car parked on the street, across the first floor to the stairs at the back, then up the stairs. The stuff wasn't heavy, but bulky and awkward, and it had taken them long enough that Jeff thought to put additional money in the parking app.

Rachel dashed around, long red hair in a pony tail, flashlight in her teeth, connecting instruments together and to the fuel cell power packs she'd brought from her lab. She'd enlisted Jeff as her lab assistant—his lack of competence in physics notwithstanding—not only because he was only one of two people to have seen whatever was that might or might not be haunting this building, but because, as she'd told him, she didn't particularly want anyone from her lab finding out about this unorthodox and unauthorized "field test."

"I'm the one here who thinks he'd seen something," Jeff said, "And

I think this is a little nuts. Don't ghost-hunters usually just use infrared cameras?" A few days before, Jeff had been brought to this two-story building in Washington Heights—a building that once housed a restaurant and pool hall and bar owned by the grandfather who'd died before he'd been born—and he thought he'd seen something.

"I'm not hunting ghosts," Rachel said. "I'm hunting entangled particles. Logical speculation from the work Carl and I've done together." Carl, her fiancé, was a neuroscientist at NYU. Rachel specialized in quantum information and quantum theories of consciousness. She and Carl had met at a conference when he suggested to her that he might have a way of trying to experimentally test her ideas.

"What we do, with live subjects, anyway," Rachel said, "is we try to entangle photons and electrons from the subjects' brains, with electrons in the detector, and then measure what happens in the detector."

She was setting up the laser emitters on the back wall, and the detector about three meters away. Trying to get where Jeff had thought he'd seen something, in the part of the building that used to be the restaurant/bar's office. The office where the World War II meat rations were circumvented. Where payoffs changed hands, where shakedowns were planned. Where numbers games were run.

Jeff worked as an Assistant Professor in Media Studies, hoping to soon be an Associate Professor. He'd never won a fistfight. He'd get guilty about the possibility of leaving out a citation. A far cry from his mother's father, who'd occupied that office.

"So, the first time we set this up," she went on, "Our jaws dropped when the detector started spitting out things that looked like EEGs. And then we went another step and tried to image, and got a few glimmers of things that looked like PET scans. If you squinted at them the right way, anyway."

Which was also the work that had gotten her tenure.

"Fine," Jeff said. "The part the boggles me is why you think shining a few lasers in an empty room is worth anything."

"I've had this wacky idea—if consciousness is a quantum phenomenon, then, maybe in the course of living, we naturally entangle some of the particles in our environment. And then maybe some echo might persist in those particles. And I've been wanting to try something like this… And if we don't get anything up here, maybe we can also try the spot where your girlfriend said she thought she saw something."

"She's not my 'girlfriend,'" Jeff said. There, in the dark, his face got hot.

Rachel was referring to Elana Roth, the woman who had first brought him to this spot. In the last week, he couldn't stop thinking about her. Probably an artifact of the adrenaline from that night, he thought. But there it was, anyway.

"Not yet, anyway," Rachel said. "This would count as, what, your second date? You're going to see her again?"

He didn't want to answer her. Instead, he changed the subject: "And where are you going to try to publish this little test?" he asked.

"*Crackpot Science Reviews,*" she said. "Or maybe *Nature Paranormal.*"

"Those—um, those don't actually exist, do they?"

She shot him a look.

"Well, what do I know about physics journals?" he said. For all he knew, there could be a *Crackpot Review.*

I mean, someone had had someplace to publish the first string theory papers... he thought.

"OK," she said. "Let's kill the lights—use the night vision glasses—stand over there, and see if you can get his attention."

Jeff put the glasses on and turned them on. He stood where he thought maybe the office door used to be, and said, "Grandpa? Jack? Jack Marcus?"

And he stood there for five minutes, trying to see another apparition, but he thought maybe the night vision goggles might have been in the way. Nothing apparent to Jeff happened.

Finally, Rachel said, "OK—I think we've got as much as we're going to get. I'm going to turn on the lights—take off the goggles—and let's pack up. I'll take a look at the tape and see if anything other than some mice scurrying by happened."

Three Weeks Before

It all began with an unexpected visit. "Are you Jeff Bernstein?" The woman stood in the office doorway. Tall, slender. Hazel eyes, light brown wavy hair tied back. She wore calf-high boots, an A-line brown skirt, a silk blouse, and the air of authority. Jeff thought he recognized her, and had a guess as to who she was.

"That's what it says on the door," he said. "And you are?"

"Elana Roth," she said. She put the jacket she was carrying over the back of his guest chair.

I was right, he thought. I did know who she is. He said, "Brooklyn Heights. City Council. What brings you all the way up here to Columbia?"

"May I sit down?" she asked, nodding slightly at the two chairs in front of his desk.

"Oh, sure," he said. He was still sufficiently surprised that someone like her would have come all the way up to Morningside Heights—instead of simply calling or emailing. Jeff taught in the Journalism school, as an Assistant Professor in Media and Politics. Every other year, he taught a class on New York City politics—since the major city elections took place on off-years.

64

She sat. "I wanted to come up to see you personally, because I wanted to discuss something personal, and off-the-record. Plus, I'm on my way uptown, and thought I might take a chance, stop in, and see if you were in."

Personal? He thought. Odd, since they'd never met before. "If you're looking for some kind of advice about something that could affect your re-election, I should mention that I can't take on any consulting at this time—due to my faculty position here."

"It's not that," she said. "Well, there's an outside possibility that someone could… Anyway, also, I'm not just running for re-election, I'm running for City Council Chair."

"Should I know that?"

"Maybe you should—it's not really announced officially, but it's also not been really a secret. Anyway, I wanted to meet you because for a long time, I've had an interest in genealogy. And it looks like my grandfather and your grandfather crossed paths in the 1940s."

"Which grandfather?" he asked.

"Jacob Marcus—I think he was known as Big Jack?"

Jeff nodded. His mother's father—the one that died before his parents had even met. The one for which he was named. "I can see why you might not want to discuss that in writing," he said.

She smiled, and nodded. "My grandfather was Abe Roth. They, um, 'worked together' in Washington Heights and the Grand Concourse in the 40s and early 50s. Anyway, it wasn't only that I was looking into my tree, but, being in City Hall, I also learned that one of their um, common interests—a building on 181st and Wadsworth—is going to be demolished in a few months. Seems someone wants to build a big new movie theater there."

"Why, what's there now?"

"A pair of defunct department stores," she said. "At the time, though, it was a restaurant on the street level, with a pool hall over it. Thought you might be interested to see it before it disappears."

So some woman just shows up at your office?" Rachel asked. "Who was this she?"

Jeff looked at her over his chicken and broccoli. They met for dinner at the Chinese restaurant across Broadway from the campus.

Even though they were in very different departments, Rachel had been one of the first other faculty members to really welcome Jeff when he first got to campus. She'd arrived at Columbia the year before Jeff. At the end of the last semester, she'd made tenure—she'd been promoted to Associate Professor in the Physics department, where she specialized in quantum mechanics and quantum information—entanglement—also, she was doing work on quantum theories of consciousness.

Jeff, in theory, would be up for tenure this year—after the close of the semester in May.

When, coincidentally, Rachel would be getting married. Not a surprise, really, Jeff thought, that she'd had it so easy finding someone. She had bright green eyes, a ready smile, and a quick laugh. Plus, as a woman working in physics, the numbers were in her favor.

"She's a City Councilmember from Brooklyn. Not sure, really, exactly, what her story is. Running for Speaker."

"You think there's more to it—more than simply what she said?" Rachel asked.

"It's just odd," Jeff said. "For someone to come all the way up in person to see me, about a minor thing like our grandfathers, when she's never even met me before, and without any reason whatsoever to think that I might have any interest in genealogy or in a grandparent who died before my parents even met."

"Well, when you put it that way…" Rachel toyed with a crab leg. "Or maybe she saw that profile of you that your friend Stu posted on his blog. That 'under-the-radar political bachelors' piece."

"Actually, maybe, but not in the way you mean," Jeff said. "That is, rather, maybe that's how she found me on the web." He speared a broccoli stalk and bit the head off.

"What's she look like?" Rachel asked.

Jeff almost gagged on the broccoli. "What?"

"What did she look like? I'm guessing that she must be around our age, give or take, if your grandparents were contemporaries."

"She was tall," Jeff said, shrugging.

"'Tall'. Right. You're going to make me Google her, aren't you? She's a public figure, there's got to be a picture on the web somewhere—probably her campaign site." Rachel reached for the tablet computer she had in her bag.

"Oh, come on," Jeff said. "Is that necessary?"

"I'm going to find out one way or the other," she said. "You might as well tell me."

"OK, fine. Apart from being tall, she had hazel eyes and dark hair. That enough?"

"She single?"

"Almost certainly not."

Rachel leaned across the table. She narrowed her eyes and peered at Jeff. "Why do you say that?"

"Because. She's attractive and she seems smart. And this is New York. So, ergo, she can't be single."

Rachel rolled her eyes. "Keep thinking like that," she said, "and you're sure not to have a date for the wedding."

Three days later

After a cryptic message from Elana, Jeff took the 2 Train to Fulton Street, and found himself waiting in City Hall Park. He was looking north toward City Hall when he heard her voice from his other side.

"Hey. I got you Starbucks. Didn't know what you wanted in it, so I got black, with sugar, sweetener, and half-and-half," she said. She sat on the bench next to him, handing him the cup and a bag with the promised packets. She took a sip from her cup. "Look, I'm going to get right to it," she said. "Still off the record. I want to ask you to come with me to that building in Washington Heights I mentioned the other day."

OK, he thought. Getting right to the chase is fine. Going to some abandoned store in Washington Heights, though? "Look," he said, "I'm afraid I don't really share your passion for genealogy. I don't really feel any pull to go up there." For one thing, Jeff really wasn't interested, particularly, in that part of the family history. For another, when he did think about it, he didn't think that someone like "Big Jack" would think much of his namesake grandson.

"You have no interest in knowing where you come from?" she asked.

"You wouldn't find it at least interesting?"

"From what I do know, I don't think I would like knowing the details," he said.

"Yeah, well," she said. "Look at me—a member in good standing of the city government. Running for the third most powerful post in the city, and one that requires the votes of my peers on the Council, at that. A gangster grandfather doesn't necessarily reflect well on me, either."

"Not inconsistent with New York City government, though," Jeff said. "Tweed and Plunkett, to name just two."

"Exactly the point," she said. "You know the history of city politics. You also know that many in the media don't feel constrained with avoiding guilt by association. That's why I've kept all of this as quiet as I can."

Interesting, Jeff thought, wasn't expecting that answer. He looked at her, more closely. She had her suit jacket draped over her crossed knees. She was wearing designer sunglasses—not knockoffs, but no one of the "name" designers. She delicately sipped her coffee.

"OK, look," she said, "I know how this will sound, but I went up there. And it was very… well, very weird. It was still late afternoon when I went up there, but it felt dark. And cold. And I got one very strong feeling that I wasn't wanted there. And another that you were."

Alone in an empty building? "OK, I can see how an empty building up there could be a little creepy, and why you wouldn't want to go back up there alone," he said. "But I would assume that there's someone else you could ask?"

"Such as?"

"I don't know. Significant other? Bodyguard?"

"We don't get bodyguards, actually," she said. "Police escort when we need it, but it wouldn't be right to try to use them for this. And I dumped my last so-called 'significant other' months ago when it turned out he grew up with Richard French."

"Richard French, the Deputy Mayor?" Jeff asked.

"The same," she said. Her phone rang. She looked at it, and said, "I'm sorry, I have to take this. Could I ask you to wait a few minutes?"

"Sure," Jeff replied. He reached for his own phone, where he found a text from Rachel. "How's coffee?"

"She asked me to go to the bldg w/," he texted back.

"And?"

"Y?"

"1ngle?"

"Y, turns out."

"GO (idiot)"

That last comment from Rachel struck Jeff as odd. Rachel had never taken that much of an interest in his love life before.

"Do you remember anything about your father's restaurant?" Jeff asked his mother on the phone. He'd rarely discussed the grandfather he'd never met with her. He knew a little about him, and thought, from what he knew, that if he'd lived, he'd be disappointed in his grandson. There he was, middle of the twentieth century; a man known by his physical size and strength, entrepreneur, reputed to be active in the Jewish mob. And here Jeff was; a bookworm who never quite figured out how to fight. And whose legal transgressions amounted to a once swiping a pack of gum, a speeding ticket, and some underage drinking and other assorted minor indiscretions.

While he had mom on speakerphone, he was also searching the web, trying to see if he could find any kind of mention of the Paladium in the newspaper.

"It was expensive," she said. "Lots of famous people would go to dinner there. Your uncle once told me that they were one of the only places in the city that could get steak during the war."

"I just found some kind of mention from the 1944 *Times* about some kind of kickback scheme for rations," Jeff said.

"That sounds about right," his mother laughed. "Any reason you're asking about this now?"

"I got a call from someone on the City Council that they're going to demolish the building it was in," he said. "I thought I might want to take a look at it. Just that I didn't know anything about it."

"I wonder why a City Councilman would even be aware of it," she said. "You know who this person is?"

"Her name's Elana Roth," Jeff said.

"Oh. If she's asking about that, then I am guessing she must be related to Abe Roth," his mother said. "That would be the most likely connection."

"She said she's his granddaughter. She said they knew each other—that they were partners of some sort."

"I think they were," she said. "I met him a few times before your grandfather died. Your uncle Max said dad and Abe had been good friends—he used to call him Uncle Abe—until he died, and then your grandmother lost touch with him."

The sun was just going down, and the lights coming up in the buildings around when Jeff saw Elana coming out of the 1 Train subway on Wadsworth and 181st Street. That is, the lights were going up in all the buildings except the one in front of him. The windows were boarded up, and pasted over with photocopies of the building permits.

Am I underdressed for exploring an abandoned building? he thought, as he watched her approach. He was in old jeans, sneakers, a T-shirt, and old leather jacket. She wore a long brightly colored dress, and carried a light jacket and a bag.

"Flashlight?" she asked, handing him a small but bright LED flashlight.

"Good idea," he said. "Wish I'd thought of that."

"Yeah—they took the lights out. It's pretty much gutted inside." She took out a key ring and opened the door. "Bottom floor used to be the restaurant. The pool hall was upstairs."

"What was it most recently?"

"Clothing on the bottom floor, sporting goods upstairs. They wanted to take all the fixtures out before demolishing the place and clearing the lot."

They walked into the building, and they both turned on their flashlights. "Creepy," Jeff said.

"No kidding," she said.

"So," she said, "I first started seeing things over there"—she waved her flashlight toward the left. "And then again in the back, near the stairs that go to the next floor." They took tentative steps further into the building.

"By the way," she asked. "What's the story with you and your friend the physics professor—what's her name, Flynn?"

"Rachel?" Jeff replied. "She's getting married in about six weeks. They even were able to book St. Ignatius of Loyola for it. Why?"

"I'd heard some things," she said. "Nothing else?"

Not for lack of trying, once, Jeff thought. "She wasn't ever interested in anyone who wasn't Catholic." He changed the subject. "What did you see upstairs?" he asked.

She laughed. "Oh, I never made it upstairs," she said. "I was so freaked out by what happened down here, I ran."

"What do you think, should we go up there?"

"Um, let's see how it goes," she said.

They walked over to the left, and Jeff stood looking at the boarded-up window. The store's façade had been new, and with the structure gutted, he could make out on the floor where the old wall used to be. For a moment, almost as out of the corner of his eye, he could almost see what the restaurant windows might have looked like. And then he heard Elana gasp.

"Did you see that?" she asked.

"What did you see?" he said.

"I thought I saw a corpse, lying on the floor."

"Really?" he said. "I thought I might have seen the windows of the restaurant." The whole space was a wide open, dark lot. Broken only by the revealed structural beams holding up the ceiling. He pointed the flashlight around, trying to see if it could reach the corners of the building, but the beam faded out in just a few yards. Then he heard—something scratching, and maybe squeaking. Rats? He thought, and shivered. He pointed his light toward the nearest corner to find a pair of mice tugging at a stray piece of newspaper. He shivered again.

"See something?" Elana asked. She moved next to him, putting her head next to his, maybe, he thought, to try to see what he could see.

"Mice," he said, "I think."

"Oh," she replied, nonchalant. "That's all."

"Let's go and see what's upstairs," he said, and started walking toward the right back corner. Elana stayed close to him. They walked about twenty paces toward the stairs when she jumped and grabbed his arm.

"What?" he asked.

"I thought I saw a beam falling at me," she said. "You didn't?"

He shook his head. He looked down at her still holding on to his arm. He thought this was a little interesting. Apparently, his looking made her embarrassed. She let go and backed away a few steps.

They walked a few more steps toward the stairs, and she jumped away, back this time.

"Something else falling?" he asked, pointing his flashlight at her.

She nodded slowly, looking ashen. "You didn't see any of these things?" she asked.

"No," Jeff said.

"You still want to try to go upstairs?"

"Yeah."

"I think maybe I'll wait outside," she said.

"Might be safer in here," he replied.

"The precinct knows I'm here—they have my phone GPS. I'll be fine. I'll wait for you outside?"

"I'll try not to be long." He pointed his flashlight toward the front door, and watched her walk out. Then he continued on toward the stairs, and then up them.

The second floor was much like the first. Beams holding up the ceiling, empty gutted floor, boarded-up windows on the north and west and north walls.

He stared at the window boards, trying to imagine how the gutted space might have looked, sixty years before. Again, almost from the corner of his eye, he thought he could almost see a bar, and pool tables. And maybe the words, spoken, "Wages of a mis-spent youth."

Jeff met Rachel for lunch a week after their trip to the haunted store.

"So I showed the tape of what we recorded at the building to Carl," Rachel said. "We inverted it, and ran it through a simulation of a whole bunch of things—PET scans, stuff like that."

"And?" Jeff asked. "Came up as so much noise, I presume?"

"Not really," she said. "Actually, it wasn't hard to map it against experimental data from all sorts of the same kinds of scans on real people. And, plus, we took some similar scans in random places, did the same kinds of tests to it. Where there were people, we got a mash-up of stuff. Where there weren't any, we got only noise."

"So you're saying something was there??"

"I would say that there were anomalous data, and that maybe there was something there. You could draw your own conclusion as to what. But I don't have a better guess," she said.

"I wonder why this would have started now," Jeff said. "I mean, there have been two generations of stores and businesses on that spot—in those buildings—since my grandfather died. No ghost stories coming out of them before now."

"Well, let's for a minute suppose that there is some sort of phenomenon going on there," Rachel said. "Just for the sake of argument. If the site had been in equilibrium for so long, and isn't now; then something changed. Something would have set it off. The question would be: What?"

"What changed?" he asked.

"Right. Not only what and where—what is it that is going on at that site, but why now and not other before?"

Jeff was listening to what she was saying. And as she was said it, he thought the obvious conclusion. "Elana," he said.

"That's the variable we know about," Rachel said. "I mean, there could be others—like the building being taken down. But given that you said that her grandfather had also been involved with the goings on there and that the deconstruction of the building had been going on for some time without any weirdness would make that a likely enough conclusion."

"She was the first one, I think, to notice anything there," he said. That was what had set off this entire chain of events, after all.

"And so you said that her grandfather and your grandfather had a relationship?" she asked.

"She said they were in the same gang. I don't really know much more than that—I don't know if she knows much more than that."

"Well, what if there was more to it than just that?" Rachel asked. "How, by the way, did your grandfather die?"

"Heart attack, at 56," Jeff said. No reason to question that, given the rest of the heart risks on that side of his family.

"Well, there's obviously some kind of link there," Rachel said. "I mean— this whole idea of a ghost aside, it seems to me that there is some sort of link between you and between your grandfathers. If it were me, I would think, just looking into that would be worth the effort."

Jeff had always been anxious about learning more about his grandfather. He was a big man—physically large, physically strong—as well as, from what he'd been told, a leader in a very tough—some would say cutthroat— "industry." And here he was—an academic, who only got exercise when he wanted it. Who triple-checked the references in his papers just to be sure that he didn't unintentionally plagiarize someone.

Jeff did not think that his grandfather, if he'd lived, would have been too impressed with his grandson.

He had on occasion dug—not very deeply—into the newspaper records to see if anything about the restaurant and bar had shown up. There were a few brief items—nothing really noteworthy. But it was possible that there was more; and as a professor in a journalism/media studies program, Jeff did have a few contacts that might know where to get more information. A few former students at the Times and the cable networks, who in turn had contacts at the NYPD and FBI. He sent out a few emails, hoping, this time, to learn something his mother and uncles couldn't tell him.

J eff thought he and Elana should meet in Rachel's office. Somewhere both private, and neutral. What Jeff had found out might explain— assuming they bought into the ghost story—what they'd experienced. In a Dybbuk sort of way. But wasn't the sort of thing likely to go down well, particularly with someone in government and with ambition… And there wasn't any easy way to reveal it.

"So, I came across a pair of documents," Jeff said.

"What kind of document? Bank records—deeds?" Elana asked.

"A Coroner's Report, and a police interview transcript," Jeff said.

"Whose?"

"My grandfather's," he said. "Things even his children never knew—I think my grandmother never knew, either."

"They did an autopsy on your grandfather, and your family didn't know?" she asked.

Because Elana would have known that for religious reasons, Jews— particularly of that generation—would not normally have approved an autopsy, and getting the coroner to do one would have required a great deal of persuading the family. Elana's question meant—how could the family not have known about it?

"Not an autopsy—just a few tissue samples," Jeff said. "I don't think anyone ever even told my grandmother."

"Why would they have even done that?" she asked.

He passed her the other packet of papers. "I dug up this—it's a transcript of a police interview. With my grandfather. About your grandfather."

"About what they were in business with together," she said. "He— what—Jack was becoming an informant?"

Jeff picked up the copy of the transcript, and flipped back through it. The details of the business—some protection, some book making, loan sharking; a few union schemes—really didn't interest him. Only the fact that he was spelling it out and naming names did. "Yeah," he said. "I don't know if what's in here was the worst of what they did—there's not a lot violent here."

"So they were looking for poisons," she said, "and suspecting Grandpa Abe. Did they find anything?"

"Not conclusively," he said, flipping through the report, looking for the right page. "But they didn't think he had had a heart attack." Which gave Jeff mixed feelings—his grandfather was probably murdered. But, on the other hand, maybe he didn't actually have a family heart disease history…

Elana looked at the two packets and the manila envelope they'd come in, and then she looked out the window. "Well, that would certainly explain why the ghost of your grandfather wouldn't be too terribly happy that I was in that building," she said. "But do you know what might have inspired him to go to the police in the first place?"

"No, not really," Jeff replied—lying. He knew very well what would have had him rethinking his life.

"Well. I guess all I can say is that I hope that whatever ugliness there was between our grandfathers," she said, "I hope that you and I—our generation—can get past it." She stood up and reached for her jacket.

"Maybe over dinner and a movie?" Jeff asked.

She looked him up and down. "I think I would like that," she said. "But I have to warn you now—so there isn't any misunderstanding down the road—my spare time might not be very spare between now and a certain Tuesday in November."

"Oh, that's OK," he said. "Part of my job is to pay attention to local races…"

"Then this might work out well," she said. She smiled, and turned, and left.

Jeff picked up the police transcript. He knew why his grandfather had turned because of the date on the transcript.

Jeff was the youngest of the cousins. The oldest cousin—his uncle's son Steve—was almost twenty years older. And the date on the transcript was just five months before Steve's birth. Maybe, instead, Big Jack had been worried about what his grandchildren would think of him. Not, so much, what he would think of his grandchildren.

Shards

aniel Wasserman almost forgot to return the salute. He'd stepped on to the station landing deck from the transport, wrinkled flight fatigues, duffle bag over his shoulder. And when he saw the Lieutenant in duty whites standing at attention holding a salute, at first, the thought did not occur that it was for *him*. Until he remembered about the silver eagles on his collar.

He stopped, dropped his bag, and returned the salute, letting the other man end his.

"Lieutenant James Parker," the other man said. He was older than Daniel—perhaps 60, give or take. A little shorter. Cropped hair ringing his head, over space-black eyes. Or maybe he wasn't that old, Daniel thought. The balding could be skewing his judgment. "Welcome to Hephaestus," Parker finished.

"Thank you, Lieutenant," Daniel said. He remembered Parker from the dossiers he'd perused in transit—Parker would be his XO. Specifically, he specialized in surface-to-orbit logistics. Not too much different than Daniel's own background in logistics generally. His big break had been during the war, organizing all of the logistics for the Venus-based assault that took Hephaestus back from the Euro-Martian alliance.

Launching the attack from Venus—where the Europeans and Martians never thought to look—had *also* been Daniel's idea. But as a commoner, there wasn't any way he'd get credit for that. He was lucky enough that his mentor, Admiral Lord Wallace, was liberal enough in outlook to take his suggestion seriously, and then give him that logistics role. For Wallace's own part, that victory had gotten him the command of the Colonial Sector. And with that role, he'd exercised his influence for a special dispensation giving Daniel a provisional promotion to Captain. Not in Solar space, of course.

Hephaestus was home to a particular sort of microorganism community. When first discovered, the biologists didn't know what to call it; it did not fit in to any of the "normal" biological kingdoms. Not bacteria, fungi, plant, or animal, but something in between plant and fungi. Like plants, they lived in part off of solar electromagnetic energy. But they also drew power from the planet's magnetic field; aided in part by their carbon-copper-silica cell walls. And they stacked on top of each other like coral, leaving the stuff behind as the communities grew.

The first humans on Hephaestus—the founders of the New Philadelphia Free Colony—realized that there was something special about the stuff: An earlier civilization had left behind huge pits where the clay-like substance had been dug up. So they sent some back to Earth, where it was discovered that when melted at 1,500 degrees and cooled into a ceramic, the material would superconduct at about 270 degrees Kelvin. Fragile stuff, ceramic wires and circuits—biggest problem on a ship in battle wasn't keeping it cool, but protecting it. Too many bad hits and your power mains would burst into a million shards.

It was possible to synthesize the material, but, as with spider silk, it was difficult to do correctly. There were other colonies with similar organisms, but none so far had the sheer amount of the material as Hephaestus.

"Can I take your bag, sir?" Parker asked.

First command decision, Daniel thought. Go the traditional imperious route? "I've carried it this far," he said. "Another few meters won't make a difference." He shouldered the bag, and they walked out of the hangar.

"How would you like to proceed, Captain?" Parker asked.

"I think I would like to get planetside as soon as convenient," Daniel said. I part because he hadn't been on a solid planetary surface for six months. He was looking forward to going for a good run on real ground in real air. But also because he wanted to see the place firsthand.

"That's unusual," Parker said. "The last commander hardly ever spent any time at all on the surface."

"I know," Daniel said. "Speaking of which, have the civilians been informed of my assuming command of the garrison?"

"In fact, no, sir. We have only just told them that Lord Captain Winstead has left."

They had been walking down a corridor lined with bulkheads. They stopped at the one with the word "CAPTAIN" glowing on the ID panel. "Here's your office," Parker said.

Daniel put his hand on the panel, and the door slid open. "Do I have one of these planetside?" he asked.

"There is a small barracks near NewPort City. But I think Lord Winstead used to stay in the Presidential Suite in the big hotel."

"When was the last time you were planetside?" Daniel dropped the duffel bag, and slid in behind the desk, and motioned for his XO to take a seat. The walls of the office gleamed with stainless steel. The desk in the middle—made of dark-stained mahogany with a brown leather chair behind it—clashed. Behind the desk, a wall-sized window framing the planet. Daniel could imagine the impression this was designed to make on a visitor. Spacious office, heavy imported desk, a noble officer in dress whites behind the desk, the AngloAmerican flag to one side, the planet behind. Designed to awe.

"Three years ago, perhaps?" Parker said. He sat, and unfolded a pad from his shirt pocket.

"That will change," Daniel said. He turned on the computer built into the desk. He noticed that there was a message waiting for him on the desktop. From Winstead, Daniel surmised. He'd read it later.

"Why should that be, Captain? Our brief is to defend the planet. Lord Winstead had always maintained that orbit was the best place to do that from."

"Do you know what happened on the surface during the Euro-Martian occupation?" Daniel asked.

"Should I?"

"You should. Everyone should. The colonists ran a spirited resistance—a great deal of nuisance campaigns initially, but when the fleet arrived, they found that the enemy forces were not in control of the surface, except in spots. You said Lord Winstead stayed at the hotel: Are there accommodations at the barracks?"

"Not really."

"OK. I'll see about getting some modest accommodations until we can get a planetside post built."

A n exhausted open-pit mine—this one already tapped out by the time humans had arrived—sat on the northwest corner of New-Port City. As part of "beautification," the city had built a running track, about 400 meters long, around the pit. Daniel ran; breathing the real air, music pouring in his ears, distracting him. He'd do at least five kilometers, or perhaps as many as seven, if he felt like it.

Each circuit held a snapshot of the city and its hundred-year history. Around the back stretch, he could see the city's towers rising out of the gray clay ash; the four orbital elevators reaching toward up; and beyond that, the broad gray expanse of so-far unmined Clay.

As he would come around the back stretch, he saw the craters and scars from the Euro-Martian bombing. And around the front side, on the other side of the pit, a few small InBot encampments. And when he looked in toward the pit, very durable industrial signs written in an alien script. So far, humans had not encountered any other living extraterrestrial cultures but had come across the remnants of a few. Several hypotheses had been floated. The one Daniel liked best was the idea that they had evolved into patterned energy; didn't need buildings and planets anymore.

The only non-terrestrial intelligence that had been directly encountered so far was, in fact, artificial. The civilization that had mined Hephaestus (and had settlements elsewhere) had left behind a race of sentient robots which someone had dubbed "InBots."

He'd finished his ninth lap when he noticed a man sitting on one of the benches. On his tenth lap, the man was still there. Odd, that, since there wasn't anything else going on, just Daniel—in civvies—running.

The man wore dark glasses, a blue light outer jacket. He sat, legs crossed, a pad on his knee. When the man was still there, looking directly in Daniel's direction, on the twelfth lap, Daniel decided to stop and see what the story was. He slowed to a walk, and approached the bench. The man rose.

"Seeing anything interesting?" Daniel asked.

"Only a new officer from Earthside," the man said. He extended a hand. "My name is Jack Mere. You must be, if I have it right, Lieutenant Commander Wasserman?"

"Jack Mere. Of Mere Freight Systems?" Daniel asked. Mere Systems ran about 40% of the freight to and from Hephaestus. The Meres were among the original settlers of New Philadelphia. The Meres and some others had left Earth for political reasons, been granted a charter, and had established a colony several kilometers away from where NewPort City would later be built.

"That's right," Mere replied.

"You must have an impressive network of contacts," Daniel said. "But your information is not completely correct. I'm a Captain." The Meres ran a fleet of freighters that moved between Earth and Hephaestus, and between Hephaestus and New Texas and Oceania. His crews would end up talking to a lot of people across AngloAmerica's interstellar holdings. He probably had a better informant network than NorthStar Network News.

"Not really," Mere said, "From what I understand your rank is as auxiliary, as you're a commoner."

Daniel tipped his head. "Technically, that's correct. However, my point still obtains. Since, as a commoner, I wouldn't be able to be a Lieutenant Commander, either."

Mere smiled, the wrinkles on the sides of his mouth folding up. "Fair enough," he said.

"I don't see a vehicle. I assume you must be headed back to the city center? Mind if I walk with you?" Daniel said.

"Heading back to the Gulch, actually," Mere replied. New Philadelphia sat in a valley—made green by the settlers—between two eroded volcanoes—that they called "the Gulch." "I told my pilot to pick me up here in about 15 minutes." He paused. "If you like, I can take you over to the Gulch. Might be interesting for you to see it. Would be interesting for us out there to see *you*. His Excellency Lord Sir Winstead never made out there. Hell, he hardly ever made it to the *surface*. And you've been here two days, and you're down here already."

"Thank you for the invitation," Daniel said. "I hope I might take you up on it another time? I think it might be best if the rest of the colony knew I was here before I start taking trips to specific parts of the planet."

"Right," Mere said. "I'd forgotten most people don't know you're even here yet. Most planetside only recently got confirmation that Winstead was finally gone. Although the *Vulcan's Hammer* had been reporting on that for months."

"The *Vulcan's Hammer?* What's that?"

"Surprises me not in the least that it was left out of your briefings," Mere said. "It's the most-read Hephaestus news site—a lot of people around here get an N3 feed; but rely on the *Hammer* for local news. Not a surprise to me, though, that Winstead wouldn't have mentioned it in his reports."

Later, back at the hotel, Daniel opened the message that had been left for him on his office desk. It read:

To my unfortunate successor:

I cannot imagine what you must have done to merit this dismal assignment. Probably it was something not quite illegal—perhaps merely dishonourable and not prosecutable. And just not quite disgraceful enough to merit expulsion from the peerage and forfeit of your title and commission.

In any case, you have my condolences. This will likely be your most distasteful posting since having to bunk with commoners during basic training (dreadful Yank custom—my apologies if you happen to be a Yank).

You will find your role here quite useless. The main approaches to the system are ably patrolled by our Navy, and so the system itself will not conceivably be under external threat.

Internal threats are quite another matter.

The locals here are a sad lot. No wonder most aristocrats want no part of this place despite the value of the Clay. On balance, the rabble here are far too radical. They do not respect their betters; they have no use for authority even after all we have done and sacrificed for their benefit. Arrogant ingrates, all. You'll do well to have as little to do with them as you can.

I would say to you, dear fellow: Keep your head down; work whatever family connections you might still have; and perhaps your exile here will be mercifully short.

You have my prayers.

Yours,

Lord Captain Sir Winston Winstead.

Well, Daniel thought. He tossed the letter into the desktop trash. Then he thought better of it and pulled it back out. Might be interesting to hold on to this.

He'd been told that Winstead had chosen to retire after a successful tenure here. This letter, together with the things that Parker had told him seemed to indicate that his information was, at best, incomplete.

He was out here, alone. His experience was in logistics; but also training in flight and flight combat. Although, as a commoner, he hadn't been allowed to fly in combat.

He needed information. He needed contacts. There was Beth Franklin who runs the *Vulcan's Hammer*. There was Jack Mere. But, he thought, those two would have particular view points. They might have good information— and they were probably worth cultivating. But he needed someone less biased.

Mere had mentioned that there was a NorthStar News beat reporter. Maybe that might work. He turned back to the computer, and started to run a search.

The following evening, Daniel sat at a table in a NewPort bar called Vesty's, sipping iced tea. Small metal tables scattered around a large, loft-like space. Floors made of stone; walls of wood. At the back, a heavy wooden bar staffed by an InBot that Daniel had been told owned the place. Except that "he" didn't look like Daniel had read InBots were supposed to look. The creatures who had made them had six limbs and four eyes and had made their robots to match (a type of "alien android," Daniel had thought). This one—and many of the others on Hephaestus—were re-making themselves to more closely resemble humans.

Meeting Ricky the InBot was already a valuable experience. More complicated and more cleverly designed than the types of robots made by humans, they were made like organisms, made, essentially, out of nanobots. These nanobots would circulate throughout their bodies; each carrying a copy of the InBot's body plan; repairing systems, metabolizing raw materials—their bodies were constantly being renewed and repaired.

Daniel sat in the bar, watching Ricky interact with the humans, and also with some of the other InBots that would wander in. If he closed his eyes, he could imagine that there were only humans in the bar; which spoke to the effort the InBots were putting into becoming "human."

But the InBots weren't Daniel's primary object today. He was waiting and watching for the NorthStar News staffer that he'd learned would hang out here. Eventually, a man in his 60s wandered in. Dressed differently than the miners and dock workers; he wore faded jeans, brown shoes, collar-less button shirt, white jacket. He walked up to the bar, and the InBot behind the bar greeted him.

"Hello, Clark. Usual?"

Clark slid on to the bar stool. "Sure," he said.

Daniel looked the guy over. *Clark*, he thought. *Clark Hamm? The guy who trashed Neil? That's the NorthStar reporter?* Daniel got up and walked out.

Daniel had still been in ROTC in college when the Euro-Martian alliance had invaded Hepheastus. Neil—Admiral Wallace—Captain Wallace at the time—had led one of the fighter wings tasked with stopping the assault by preventing the invasion force from leaving the Solar System. They'd failed—and shortly after, Clark Hamm had written a piece blaming Neil for the failure—and due only to Neil's title. The underlying theme: Neil had his command because of his title; open ranks would have led to more competent officers. While Daniel agreed with open ranks (and he had a vested interest in that), he knew, from Neil, that the invasion fleet had had such a big jump on them, that no one would have been successful in that mission. And the fact that Hamm had singled out and personally attacked Daniel's mentor pressed at his gut. At a minimum, the guy could not be trusted. After all, the material for that piece? Had come from an interview Neil had given Hamm on the eve of battle.

Three days later, Daniel was back in his office on the orbital platform. He had still not figured out the best way to introduce himself to the population, but word of his arrival had gotten out.

In his office, sitting in the chairs in front of him, Clark Hamm. And the cousin of Jack Mere, Claire. Jack had asked if Daniel would receive her. They had a complaint, and they'd taken the Elevator up to the platform.

When they walked in, Claire Mere was striding ahead of the two men. Walking as if she was in charge. She wore her brown-red hair just below the collar of her tan leather jacket. Daniel had looked her up, and knew she was in her thirties, but her bearing made her seem older.

"Please come in, have a seat. I'm Captain Wasserman." He motioned to the other guest chairs, and they all sat, three of them in the chairs on the visitor side of the giant desk. Daniel crossed his legs, and held a Pad on his knee. "So, what—"

"The government is trying to put us out of business," Claire said, cutting him off.

The obvious reaction would be to challenge this assertion. Either by simply denying it, or by asking her what she meant. Daniel had no idea what she meant, and could not imagine what mechanism the government could even use to undermine the Meres' business. But, he thought, perhaps he could try responding with a different tack. "Supposing this is true, what might you think I might be in a position to do about it?"

"So you are aware that noble family companies pay a lower tariff rate? Specifically, Kennedy shipping gets a waiver on Earth-orbit dock fees as well as a 10% break on import duties?" She asked.

"As these facts would not have a bearing on Hephaestus planetary defense, I was in fact not aware of it, I have to admit," Daniel said. "But even so, supposing I believe you; and that this is accurate; I am still unclear as to what I might be able to do about it." He looked over at Hamm, who was raptly paying attention to this exchange. Daniel didn't see any recording device (which didn't mean he didn't have something), but mostly he seemed to be absorbing everything.

Daniel's eyes met Hamm's. Hamm said, "Claire has already requested all this be off the record."

Then why's he here? Daniel wondered. This visit wasn't making much sense. Come all this way up to bring a complaint that Daniel wouldn't even be able to do anything about. And to air it in front of an Earth-based reporter.

"It's not only paying the taxes," she said, "which are inherently unfair. It's the targeting. This differential treatment makes it very difficult for us to maintain competitive pricing. And I want to bring this to your attention because you are probably *not* aware of it. And neither, either, I think, are your superiors. But what you would be aware of is the role our ships have typically played in planetary defense. And even logistics during the last war, even while Hephaestus was occupied. And maybe if you know about it, you might be able to do more about it than we can. As you're a 'disinterested party.'"

Daniel wasn't sure what to think. This was an opportunity, even before his formal introduction to the general population, to try to buy some credibility. So, he said, "Well, Ms. Mere. You came all the way up here, I presume, not just to tell me something, but to ask me for something. So, let's for the sake of argument say I accept what you're saying. Given this, what would you want from me?"

"I would want to ask you to take a look into this for yourself," she said. "And maybe ask about a few other things that have been going on out here in the Colonies."

Well, that was completely unsatisfying, Daniel thought as Lord Wallace's image faded. There *is* unfair treatment. The government—at best—doesn't care. *Probably they don't care,* he thought. Toss in a few breaks for the nobles;

and then who cares? That those breaks weren't random? No one in DC, London, or New York would care. Daniel wasn't sure *he* would have cared, were he still Earthside. Sure, the unfair advantage would sting, but it would be only one more in a long list. But posted here… As the de facto local representative of the federal government, the frustration would come down on *him*. Plus, he'd already met some of the people involved.

An idea crossed his mind, and he was reaching for the intercom to call Parker when a call request arrived, identified as Leah Franklin. He took the call.

Franklin's image appeared where Wallace's had been. "Good evening, Captain," she said. "I hope you are well."

"Thank you. I'm surprised to be hearing from you this way. I'd have thought you'd have come up."

"I might, later," she said. "This is urgent, however. Is this secure? Are you alone?"

"I am," he said. "How can I help?"

"Have you been reading the *Hammer*?"

"On occasion—I do mean to get into it more frequently—"

"I meant, today?"

"I'm sorry, Ms. Franklin, no, I haven't."

"Leah," she said. "Then can I ask you to bring up the site at vulcanshammer.hp; and then also bring up freehammer.hp."

He brought up Franklin's newspaper; entered his credentials to get to the paid content (Franklin provided free access to all military personnel), and then went to the other location.

Which did not require credentials. Identical content was splashed there—free.

"Well," he said. "That's… remarkable. I assume this isn't intentional?"

"Certainly not *my* intention," she said. "Now, watch this." She typed at an out-of-view keyboard.

A new item appeared on the legitimate site: "Wanted to report that the *Hammer* has had a good first interview with the new Garrison Commander. Full interview with 3D video coming soon!"

Five seconds later, the new text appeared on the cloned site.

"I, um, can see how this would be of some concern to you," he said to Franklin.

"I bill subscribers monthly," she said. "I am already seeing cancellations."

"As if someone was trying to damage your business." One item is unique;

two are a coincidence, he thought. If there's a third... "I am not sure what I can do to help you, though. Perhaps local—"

"I would like to ask you for a favor," she said. "I would like you to tell—perhaps leak—to Clark Hamm that this is happening."

"Isn't he your primary competition at NorthStar?"

"Which means he would have complete credibility," she said.

"Assuming NorthStar isn't responsible?"

"If they wanted my business, they'd try to buy it—perhaps using not entirely aboveboard means—but they'd want the value intact, not diminished this way."

She had a point there. "I will see what I can do," he said. "You probably won't hear from me directly, however—whatever I might be able to do would be unofficial."

"I understand Captain. And thank you." And she hung up.

Daniel slumped back in his chair in the darkened room. The light from the planet streaming in through the window behind him, with the office lamps off, was nearly all the illumination in the room. He rubbed his chin. Franklin had a point. Assuming NorthStar wasn't responsible, Hamm would have unassailable credibility.

But he might not be the only one, Daniel thought. What if there was someone else—someone else with credibility, with contacts...

Most of the settled parts of Hephaestus were gray. The human settlers had found them that way: The previous owners had ripped up much of the surface, mining clay. When humans first arrived, they found InBots—in their original configurations—still tending equipment around idled open-pit clay mines. Until the lab results had come back from Earth, the first settlers had initially ignored the mines, assuming they'd been exhausted. They'd come seeking a fresh start, not resources. So they'd built and greened the gulch—formally known as the New Philadelphia Free Colony. It was now the largest stretch of inhabited green anywhere on the planet.

Maybe because none of the residents work *here*, Daniel thought. He'd stepped out of his fighter on to spongy green moss. They'd made a flat landing area—mostly used as an ioncopter pad. A few feet away, in every direction, grew low bushes. Beyond them, trees. Presumably, nestled among the trees, the houses.

Jack and Claire Mere met him there at the field. Looking at them—uncle and niece—together, he could see the family resemblance. Claire was shorter; blonde. Jack stood almost two meters, thin, brown hair. But they had the same angles in their eyes and cheekbones.

"Captain Wasserman. Thank you for accepting my invitation," Jack said, holding out his hand.

Daniel shook it. "Thank you for the invitation. The landscaping work you've done here in your niche is quite impressive."

"'Gulch'," Claire said.

"It takes a fair amount of work," Jack said. "We do some ourselves; we hire InBots to do some of the rest."

"By the way, how does that work?" Daniel asked, "InBots and the local economy?"

"Almost all of them decided to act like humans," Jack said. "So we treat them that way. They pay local taxes; they vote—everything. Been that way for 150 years. But let's head to the house—it's just beyond the trees."

The Mere's house stood two stories, made of prefabricated carbon fiber/polymer composite and glass. Except for the floors made of hard blonde maple in parallel planks. The three of them sat down around a small round table in the living room, near a widow facing that vertical line of oak and maple.

"I have a favor to ask," Daniel said. He hoped he wasn't being too abrupt. He wanted to avoid pretense by bringing up business only at the end of the visit. "I am hoping that your vast network of contacts might be able to find a particular piece of information for me."

"Why do you think we have some sort of spy network?" Claire asked.

"I didn't say 'spy,'" Daniel said. "And you did know I was arriving to take command here when most of your neighbors didn't even realize that Winstead had been sacked."

"We—our crews, anyway—found out about that in Earth space," Jack said. "It didn't seem to be hidden; it seemed to have been openly discussed on Earth."

"Right. Exactly. You have ships going to all corners of AngloAmerican holdings—maybe even to the Southern Block or Asian colonies, too. And so you hear things."

"Fair enough," Jack said. "So what is it you think we might be able to hear for you, Captain?"

"I assume you are familiar with *Vulcan's Hammer?*"

Jack and Claire looked at each other.

"Everyone reads the *Hammer*," Claire said.

"Everyone subscribes?" Daniel asked.

"We all do," Claire said, waving an arm to indicate the gulch.

"My understanding is that pay-per-view is more popular among the miners and InBots," Jack added.

Daniel took out a pad, and went to freehammer.hp. He handed the pad to Jack.

"That's remarkable," Jack said. "How did you find out about this?"

"I am not entirely free to say," Daniel replied. "I can say that this was brought to my attention as a complaint. And while it is not entirely clear that this would fall under military jurisdiction, I do feel inclined to help, if I can. In any case, I do need to look into this in the event that it does fall under my responsibilities."

"So I take it you would like me to ask around," Jack said.

"That's the long and short of it."

Jack and Claire looked away from Daniel and at each other.

"I think you might not have the best person," Jack said. "If I could; I would suggest you talk to Clark Hamm. He's a correspondent that NorthStar News sent to keep an eye on us. He usually knows what's going on…"

"Not that you would know it by the reports they run on NorthStar," Claire said.

"Right. But he's got a finger into a lot of things going on in NewPort. He'd probably be your best bet, if there is something to be dug up."

Daniel leaned back and stroked his chin. He didn't like Hamm. Or, he presumed he didn't. Ham's history with Lord Wallace was one thing. Another was the arrogance with which Daniel thought Hamm had stood, when Daniel saw him at the bar. Although, now, three people he was coming to respect had made the same suggestion. "I intend to consult him, as well," he said. "And I will also make use of my own resources. But in any case, for any finding to have meaningful weight, it would be best if it could be corroborated from at least two independent sources."

Daniel had set up a command post in one of the downtown hotels—the owner had insisted. Daniel had first set up a Prefab Landing Encampment just outside of town, where the highways and levi-rail converged on the approach to the orbital elevator. The NewPort residents thought this odd. But to Daniel it made perfect sense to set up a command base at a logistically-sensitive spot. In any case, the NewPort Regal offered a suite and adjacent rooms for free; and Daniel felt it would be rude to turn them down. So he moved most of his day-to-day functions and links there.

He sat at the desk in the converted suite living room, Lieutenant Parker sitting across from him. "In your experience here, Parker, who would you think would have the capacity to steal entangle-locked transmissions?"

"The only way you could do it," Parker said, "and this isn't something I'm expert at. But you could tap it at the gap between the entangled sets and the conventional optical switches."

"So someone could get at it by getting at the switch feed?"

"Right. You'd get there, and then re-distribute it on a parallel network. Meantime the original signal would get copied and sent out on the quantum pipe like normal, and no one would know," Parker said.

"And the time delay?"

"If it was automated, probably, a few seconds."

"Which tracks," Daniel said. "Next question: Who would I ask about Internet pipes on Hephaestus?"

"That's easy, sir. There is only one pipe in or out, for security."

Daniel rubbed his eyes. "Let me guess. It's military; on our station. And we make it available for civilian use."

"Yes, sir. Unrestricted, unlimited, and free of charge."

"Do you realize, Lieutenant, that this implicates us here?"

Parker nodded. "Yes, sir. Also, Franklin knew this; she may have assumed you did too."

So why ask me to investigate? Daniel thought. *If she knew—if she knew what I'd find, then she'd want me to find it.* "Most likely, the perpetrators are military," he said. "Not me, not, I would guess, ordered by Winstead. Can I assume you're not involved?"

"No, sir," Parker said. "For one thing, officer unique ID sigs would be all over everything—it'd be flagged immediately."

"Right," Daniel said. An anti-espionage matter reserved for especially sensitive sites. And as the last war had been fought in large part over Hephaestus, this installation counted as sensitive. "No officers. Enlisted, then." He paused. "MPs?"

"Military Police?" Parker said. "Would seem a bit unlikely, don't you think, sir?"

"Certain MPs would have the training to do it," Daniel said. "And on duty they'd have the authority to access almost anything they wanted—" Marine MPs on duty carried the effective rank of Colonel—"but without leaving a unique officer ID sig."

"They'd leave the station MP sig," Parker said.

"Right. So let's look for that—we'll have to do it ourselves—to confirm.

But that won't bring us any closer than we already are. We'll have to conduct a surreptitious investigation, and without the use of our law enforcement personnel..."

D aniel chose to wear civvies to meet with Hamm. He'd asked for a meeting at Vesty's—someplace public. He'd set the meeting for early evening—about an hour before the first mining shift would be coming off the clock. So the place should be mostly empty, and quieter than usual. But late enough so that the meeting would be time-limited.

Hamm was already waiting when Daniel walked into the bar. He was sitting at one of the bistro tables near the bar, sipping something honey-colored, with ice. Single malt, Daniel guessed.

Daniel walked over, and slid on to the other stool. A half-converted InBot waiter came over, and Daniel ordered an iced tea. By Hamm's breath and manner, Daniel concluded that the glass in his hand wasn't his first.

"You rang, sir?" Hamm said.

"You come highly recommended," Daniel said. "It has been suggested that you would might have insight into some of the goings on around here."

"Not that my employer would know," he said.

"I'm not your employer," Daniel said. "I've got a different perspective."

"But you still don't like me."

Perceptive, Daniel thought. They'd met once, and he'd tried to be careful not to betray an opinion one way or the other. "What makes you say that?"

"I know that half the planet has been suggesting that you meet me. But it's taken you this long to actually do it. You have another conclusion?"

"OK," Daniel said. "Then if you'd like to know why, then I have a question for you."

"Shoot."

"What do you have against Admiral Wallace?"

"Nothing in particular," Hamm said. "And I would say that I never realized that Wallace held a grudge from that piece. From years ago. But one of the things that drives cutting journalism is outrage. And as a commoner—like you, I might observe—I sometimes get outraged about the preferential stuff that aristocrats get. And it stings more, that it didn't used to be that way. And Lieutenant Wallace, at the time, was made a squadron leader when he wasn't the best pilot. And I meant to suggest that part of the reason we lost the first war—lost *this* place to the Euros in the first place—was crap like that. And, yeah, it irked me."

Except, of course, Daniel owed almost every career opportunity he'd had to Neil Wallace. Without his patronage, Daniel's suggestion for using Venus as a staging area would never even had gotten heard. And no other flag officer would have put a commoner in charge of the logistics on Venus. Or pulled strings and called in favors to get Daniel *this* posting and the equivalent rank it carried. "So, how is it, you think, that a common-born like me got posted here?"

"Wallace?"

"I have a difficult time believing the portrait you've painted," Daniel said. "Since for my whole career he has opened doors for me that most in his position would have just as soon left closed."

Hamm's eyes widened. "Interesting. Maybe he learned something from that experience. But, you said you had something?"

"Something I could give you. But I have a question first." Daniel took a swig of his iced tea. "Does NorthStar see the *Hammer* as competition?"

"*I* see it as competition," Hamm said. "At least, for news on and from here. But, personally, I do OK in getting stuff. My problem is with getting what I find past my boss and out on to the nets. And given how, um, 'editorially filtered' our reportage from here is, I would have to say, no. If N-cubed wanted this market, we'd be doing a better job. Also, we're ad-driven. And if there was more money in advertising here, Leah Franklin wouldn't be charging subscription fees in the first place."

Daniel rubbed his chin. He opened the *freehammer* site on his pad; it was as he thought he'd remembered: No ads. So Casey and Jackson weren't doing it for ad money. Although, he thought, who on Hephaestus would by ads on the bogus site, anyway? "Money aside," he said, "in your expertise, who would have a motive to be undermining the *Hammer?*"

Hamm swirled his drink, ice clinking against the glass. "Someone with resources who doesn't like what the *Hammer* publishes?" he said.

"Seems, from the little time I've been on-planet so far, that most of the people with the resources *like* what they do," Daniel said.

"Except—"

"Except?"

"Well, except for *you guys*—the government," Hamm said. "The *Hammer* caused all kinds of problems for Winstead; arguably got him yanked back Earthside; they published details about a lot of the hidden fees and extra taxes that the Feds had passed on us. Led to some, um, uncomfortable confrontations between us—I mean the locals—and Winstead and his garrison."

Hamm went on. "The Mere's and a few of the others out at the Gulch still have some contacts and pull back home and got the Feds to defuse the situation by yanking Winstead and pulling some of the fees. But it caused them a headache." He paused. "Responsible for you're being here, too, I guess."

"And the government cannot take retaliatory action against a publication," Daniel said.

"Well, they could *try*," Hamm said. "But before she moved out here, in a prior life, Leah Franklin was a lawyer back home. I think she told me she spent a lot of time with 1st and 56th Amendment issues; she was some kind of media lawyer. So she'd be in a good spot to look after her own interests, if the Feds came after her that way. Plus she still knows other big shots back home, if she needed help."

Daniel nodded slowly. Arrows pointed toward the Federal government, possibly intentionally trying to drive the *Hammer* out of business. Already, he was composing a rather forceful set of questions and comments for his next debriefing. "OK. Here is what I am going to tell you. This will shortly be entered into public military records, but not widely released, and it cannot be known that you learned this from me. However, two privates—Military Police—have been taken into custody. We found them tapping the *Hammer's* feed at the quantum-optical switch gate on the Station."

Hamm sat up straighter. He pushed his drink away and took a small pad out of his jacket pocket. "You're kid—you're not kidding. Can I see them?"

"Probably you cannot see them. You can try through normal channels, but I suspect that this issue may soon no longer be in my hands. And I could not give this information directly to the *Hammer* since they would not have objectivity. Will you be able to get this information published?"

Hamm shrugged. He wasn't looking at Daniel anymore, but tapping furiously at his pad. "Probably not," he said, "Not on N-cubed, anyway, not if this is something the government would find embarrassing. But I can try… And I can 'leak' my report out locally—something I do all the time…"

I see from your report that you have detained these two MP Privates." Lord Wallace said. He tossed the pad he was reading from on the desk in front of him.

Daniel stood, back against the window (curtain closed), standing before the holographic representation of his commanding officer and the image of his office back in Virginia. "Yes, sir. Theft is still against the UCMJ, last I checked."

"In fact it is," Wallace said. "And what disturbs me is not the arrests, but what I've heard of their defense."

"That disturbs me, too, sir." The two MPs, after consulting with a JAG lawyer, maintained admitted to tapping into the *Hammer's* feed at the switchboard; but they claimed to be acting on orders. Daniel intended to find out the truth about this claim from Wallace.

"Well, Captain. I can assure you that this order did not come from this office." Wallace paused. "And, personally, I hope that you will accept that. I hope that you know that, after our length of service together, I would never have kept something of this magnitude or sensitivity from you."

His cheeks burned. He tried to calm himself, so as not to show it (even if the holographic system tended to not be exactly precise with color). No, it's not that the AngloAmerican government would never give such an order.

Not even that his mentor would never pass on such an order. No. Only that Wallace *wouldn't leave him in the dark about it*. And while, Daniel thought, there was some value—some interpersonal value there, it wasn't enough. Not to overcome this. "Are those valid orders?" he asked, trying to keep his voice level.

"I don't yet know," Wallace said. "I have some enquiries going up the line. But I would suspect, and warn you in advance, there might seem to be a high likelihood that they are authentic. I do not know if I should like to call them 'legitimate', as military orders for Hephaestus are supposed to go through this office, and these did not."

Message: The two MPs, Casey and Jackson, are telling the truth. And the Federal Government is trying to undermine a publication it doesn't like. As he was trying to think of what to say next, Wallace said, "Captain, I am switching to protocol Boston 328. Please match settings."

"Boston 328" was their code for an encrypted cipher they used during some of the more sensitive logistics planning on Venus. Not merely encryption, it would also write over the transmission record with an intelligently rendered image and sound script. No one should know that what was in the official log wasn't what was actually said.

"Danny," Wallace said, playing on familiarity.

What was coming wasn't going to be good.

"I know you well enough by now to know that you're almost certainly angry about this."

"I can't see why anyone might be *angry* about something like this," Daniel said. It was not *only* the issue of subverting the Constitution; but that he'd been set up. If he believed Neil, then, they'd *both* been set up.

Wallace waved a hand. "You should know that to some extent, I share it. For one thing, as I've said, this didn't come from me; I don't know if this was pre-existing order from just before I took over this sector from Duke Sydney. Most likely it wasn't; and they kept me—as well as you—out of the loop because if they had told me, I *would* have told you."

"And the Constitutional issues?"

Wallace shook his head. "The way to deal with rabble-rousing is to counter it with truth, fact, logic. Sometimes ridicule. Not ham-handed suppression. That can never work; usually makes the problem bigger. Especially once it gets out."

"I believe it will get out, and quickly, too," Daniel said.

"Right," Wallace said. "Well. When it gets out. You will likely find yourself the target of a great deal of local anger and local political pressure. I would want to remind you that your mission for me and the most critical strategic interest for our Nation, is to safeguard the Clay supply for AngloAmerica. Which means also safeguarding it *from the local colonists*, if necessary."

"Most likely, I will be seen as the representative of the government that did this," Daniel said. "Which may make that mission somewhat complicated."

"I understand that," Wallace said. "No one said this mission was *easy*. But I will try to see what sort of interference I can run for you on this end. At a minimum, I expect, these two MPs will be thrown out the exhaust. I do have some substantial pull here—winning the war brings some privileges—and I will see if what I can do about getting someone with a commission similarly ejected. And I will get credit attached to your name; that, at least, should help for now."

Wallace waved his hand, signalling that they were switching back to normal channels. And after a few more exchanges, centering mostly on routine business (and back on the record), Wallace dismissed him, and they closed the connection.

Daniel turned to face the window. The sun was setting; lights coming up. Maglev rail cars brought Clay ore in toward the depot, and elevator cars sent it up to the Station. In the sunset, Daniel could almost make out the strand connecting the Station to the surface, strung with cars on their way up.

Partly, Wallace was right—he *was* outraged at what was happening here.

As a commoner, one expected to run into roadblocks; this was how the aristocracy had created itself in the first place. Over the last 200 years, they'd bought their way in, first to the U.S. Congress, and then into the titled nobility after the Great Reunification. They passed laws designed to give themselves economic advantages; designed to keep upstarts down. As time went on, these became even more rigid. And that's how things were on Earth.

But part of the promise of coming out here, and to the other colonies, was to get away from that. People came out here for a fair shot, without running up against the advantages the aristocrats had arranged for themselves.

On the other hand, as Wallace had made clear, Daniel had a mission; and orders to follow and an oath of office to uphold. To navigate this strait, he'd need a plan. And the only way to build a plan was to work backwards from the desired result.

The hotel gave Daniel the use of one of the larger conference rooms. He'd asked them to configure it theater style, with a lectern at the front and audience seating facing it. He would come in after everyone else was seated, make a statement, and take questions.

He looked to see who was already there. Hamm. Franklin. The Meres; about two thirds of the Colony Council. And a few others were monitoring. Including TransSolar News, Le Galaxie, and one or two others from Mars and the Southern Block. He walked in, going to the lectern. His statement:

"By this time, the facts surrounding the illegal re-posting of content from the *Vulcan's Hammer* are likely known to you. The biographical details of Privates Casey and Jackson will be provided to you upon request, as well as details about the charges and evidence against them—as much as we can make public prior to trial. Casey and Jackson claim to have been acting under orders. A Navy JAG investigation has found evidence that they did receive unauthorized communications from officers under Admiral Duke Jane Sydney's command. I want to make clear, however, that at this time Admiral Lord Wallace has sole authority for military orders in this sector, and any orders coming from Admiral Duke Sydney's office ought have no authority. This investigation is ongoing. I am ready for your questions."

Clark Hamm raised a hand. "Captain; will the *Hammer* be compensated?"

"Possibly," Daniel said. "This is also still under consideration."

Claire Mere raised a hand. "I realize I'm not media."

"We won't stand on ceremony here," Daniel said.

"OK, then. I have a question on a different topic. I don't know if you may have seen, Kennedy Shipping gets preferential treatment on the routes between 'Phaestus and Earth. What will you do about that?"

If Daniel hadn't thought that someone—he had actually thought it would be Franklin—was going to ask that, he'd have been rather angry. It was meant to embarrass either him or the government. It was off-topic. And, if he had been unprepared, it would have reflected poorly on both him and on the government. As it was, he had a response. "Not a problem to ask something off the announced topic, Claire," he said. "I have seen evidence to that effect. Unfortunately, in official channels, I am required to mention that this is not, strictly, a military issue, and I have no direct influence on such matters. I have raised this with my superiors, but they, also, are military and have no direct influence over political matters."

The Meres looked at each other, and exchanged looks with the few others from the Gulch.

Behind the lectern, Daniel tapped a note on his pad for Claire and Jack.

"Other questions?" he asked.

Leah Franklin: "How much time will you be spending on the surface, verses orbit?"

"Thank you. I actually intend to establish a primary command base on the surface. I am going to order most of my command staff to relocate here as well, as well as most of the Marine complement. Also half the garrison fighter squadron will be land-based. Next question?" With no other questions, Daniel closed the briefing.

He walked to his office, where the Meres were already waiting in the hallway for him. "Come in," he said, inviting them in. "Have a seat."

"Interesting performance," Jack said. "You've done one heck of a balancing act. But you have to know that it's untenable."

"I've got another bit of balancing," he said. He gave Jack a data chip. "I can't myself fix the bit with the taxes and Kennedy. What I can do, though, is authorize the procurement of local services. All Hephaestus defense logistics will be going through Mere Shipping. I can't give you a contract because that would require ratification; but I can make one-off purchases, which I will do."

"Thank you, Captain Wasserman," Jack said. "I wish you luck with your balancing act." And they left.

Daniel slid in behind his desk, checking his messages, and checking the newsfeeds. He noticed on the *Hammer*—the full pay site, the stolen site was gone—that Clark Hamm had left NorthStar, and had become an opinion blogger for the *Hammer*. His inaugural post was about the Kennedys and the Meres and the tax laws. Daniel thought it likely that Hamm's perspective was likely to be popular on Hephaestus.

The hammer fell six months later, and came in the form of a summons from Admiral Duke Sydney. Mostly, these months had gone smoothly. True, Clark Hamm bloviated regularly from his new perch at the *Hammer*. And the Meres and other Gulch residents kept lobbying him. He didn't mind—he found them all, to a one, articulate and intelligent. While he had some sympathy for their points of view—and in particular, that the government should keep the commitments it made in the Gulch's Charter, he could not bring himself to their perspective. But they kept trying. Jack Mere seemed to think that all it would take would be time, and a precipitating event.

Eventually, Neil started skipping their weekly briefing. Finally, one Tuesday afternoon, the holoprojector came on. But standing before Daniel stood Admiral Duke Sydney, not Neil.

"Good tidings, Acting Captain Wasserman," Sydney began. She was tall; slightly pudgy with her mostly grey hair tied in a bun. "You are hereby ordered to appear in person, on my flagship, at coordinates being sent to you on a subchannel."

"Sir, yes sir. I shall confirm with Admiral Wallace—"

"That will not be necessary, Acting Captain. Admiral Wallace has been reassigned. I am now in charge of the Colonial Sectors. As such, I am now your commanding officer. You will take your captain's yacht, as soon as possible, to the rendezvous coordinates where we will meet aboard my ship, the *Audacious*."

Neil's been 'reassigned'! he thought. *For running interference for me,* he wondered. And the Duke ultimately responsible for a great deal of the unrest was now back in charge. And Sydney wanted him in a small boat, not in a fighter. This was a signal. "Should I plan on taking the captain's yacht back, after?"

"I had heard you were clever and perceptive," Sydney said. "Impressive. We can use you, I think, remaining on Hephaestus. The answer to your question, and I think, also your implied question. Yes, you would plan on returning to your command in the yacht."

"Sir, yes sir. I will report as ordered. Anything else, Admiral?"

"Not over an open channel," Sydney said. "Looking forward to meeting you in person."

Daniel was less than a light year from the *Audacious*, when he picked up another signal—another yacht-sized craft, moving to meet him.

Should be called the Arrogance, Daniel thought, referring to Sydney's flagship. He checked the incoming yacht's ID beacon, and didn't recognize it. But as it came with an AU, the beacon flipped, and the computer registered it as the personal ID of Admiral Lord Wallace. Shortly thereafter, Neil called in.

"Permission to rendezvous, Captain?" he asked.

"Did not expect to see you out *here*," Daniel replied.

"And as far as anyone is concerned, you haven't. May I come aboard for a few minutes? It's important. And I don't want any of it registered."

Several minutes later Daniel met him at the airlock of the tube connecting the two yachts. Neil wore civvies—khaki slacks, blue button-front shirt, brown shoes. Daniel had only rarely seen his former commander out of uniform.

"Welcome aboard, Admiral," he said, holding the salute, waiting for it to be returned.

"Put your arm down, Danny, I'm not here as an Admiral."

Daniel extended his hand, instead, and Neil shook it. "I hope they haven't drummed you out?"

"They might have, if they could have," he said. "My family still has connections, too. Instead, they've bounced me back to homeland defense."

Which, Daniel knew, was meaningless. None of the major powers had ever violated the Earth Attack Ban Treaty; the psychology of the Treaty and the inevitable reprisals for violating it kept Earth safe.

"Sydney will probably tell you this," Neil said, "when you see her. Probably, she'll gloat."

They walked to the yacht's cramped galley. Daniel poured coffee. "I suspect you didn't come all this way just to tell me this?"

"Certainly not," Neil said. "But you should be warned and aware. With part of the maneuvering here, they sacked me, but in so doing, had no logical reason—except your status—to sack you. And given the nature of the colonial issues on Hephaestus, the powers that be felt that that was a bridge too far. So Sydney and Winstead are stuck with you. But, I think, they would rather like it if they weren't."

Daniel shrugged. "That's obvious," he said.

"Perhaps. What do you see them doing about it?"

"Mostly what people like that always do. Power games. Low-level harassment and micromanaging. Bureaucratic mouse-mazes."

Neil shook his head. "My sources tell me they intend to go beyond that."

"How?"

"I don't have details. I am assuming that they may employ, among other things, personal humiliation, humiliation of Hephaestus while trying to make you look responsible to the colony, revocation of colonial charters and privileges, or some combination or selection from all of these. I came out here to tell you this, to tell you also that you that this is combat; you should see it that way."

Daniel paused. What he was about to say, taken the wrong way by someone who wanted to take it the wrong way, could put him in an uncomfortable spot. "Sir," he said. "Has it occurred to you that the colonists on Hephaestus have valid complaints against the Federal Government?"

Wallace crossed his arms. "I think about that all the time," he said. "It is not only Hephaestus, although with the Clay, it is certainly the most obvious example. But colonial charters that granted old-fashioned rights are being upended. I do find it quite troubling. The thing is, Daniel, that as infuriating as this can be, that we put that aside. Even with these developments, the colonies still have it better under us than they would under anyone else. And we can—we must—work within the system. Change will eventually come."

A dmiral Duke Elizabeth Sydney had Daniel brought to a conference room near the bridge of her flagship, the *Audacious*. She wore a full dress-duty uniform, embellished with family and peerage insignias. This was not usual practice, even among the more self-conscious of the aristocracy. The Admiral invited Daniel to sit down. Odd mix there—overly formal uniform, overly familiar protocol.

"Acting Captain, it has been brought to the attention of the powers that be that you have contracted nearly all of your logistics shipping with Mere Shipping; a local Hephaestus company. Is this true?"

"Yes, sir."

"Very well. Can I presume you had a good reason for this?"

"Yes, sir."

"Right, then. I presume it had to do with keeping the local proles tranquil?"

"Something along those lines, sir," Daniel said. It would be best if he could avoid giving a detailed explanation.

"Right, then, Captain. Knowing your record, we had concluded that something like that must have been the reason. And so you will not be penalized at this point for this. However, this is not sat well with some of the other shipping companies."

Sydney looked at Daniel, waiting, apparently, for Daniel to contribute to the conversation.

Sydney continued. "Some of the more well-connected companies. And while your practice has hewed to the letter of the law, the owners of these companies are, still, quite irate. Enough so that changes were demanded.

"You should be quite grateful, Captain. Lord Wallace fell on his sword for you. He's taken responsibility, given the same explanation as you have today. And he has been reassigned to Earth Home Continent Defense. I have reassumed command of this sector. As such, I am now your Commanding Officer."

"Yes, sir."

"I have reviewed your service record. Two things become starkly apparent. You are very bright. And you have been indulged by your prior commander. That indulgence ends here. Do I make myself clear, commoner?"

"Crystal, sir." Daniel forced himself to focus on a pleasant thought— Central Park in mid-summer, for example—to try to keep his face from heating up.

"Lord Wallace expended a great deal of his personal political capital to keep you in your unusual position," Sydney said. "Not, truthfully, that anyone with a proper pedigree was interested in assuming that command. In truth, it may be suited only to one such as you. In any case, there will be new ways of doing things from this point on. Questions to this point, Captain?"

"No, sir," Daniel said.

"Very well. From this point on, military procurements aggregating over a nominal sum will need to be reviewed by me, or by someone I designate. Before you ask, yes, this means you can still buy pads and batteries without getting permission—I don't have time to do all your procurements for you. However, contracting of major services such as military shipping will need to be reviewed. That little loophole you used has now been closed.

"To that specific end, I have reviewed your use of shipping services, as you may have already guessed. You are paying too much. You are hereby ordered to cut the fees you pay to Mere by 25%. Further, you are also ordered not to use one company for all shipping. Specifically, I am ordering you to contract 35% of your shipping with Kennedy, until further notice. Questions?"

This would drive the Meres out of business. Not only will a portion of the business be pulled, but even the proportion that would remain wouldn't be enough, given these new cost limits.

If that wasn't enough, Hephaestus would just as likely see these changes as intentionally inflammatory. "May I speak candidly, sir?"

"In this case, since you might have something interesting to say about that colony, granted."

"Various advantages, viewed by the colonists as unfair, enjoyed by noble-owned companies, are a particular sore point. Many on Hephaestus believe that these advantages essentially violate their original charter. These changes may be disruptive."

"We know, I'm afraid," Sydney said. "Those charter provisions were ill-conceived to begin with. In time—and sooner rather than later—I expect that Their Majesties—or at least one of them if not both—will see fit to officially revoke those charters.

"In any case. Yes, we expect disruptions. It is your job to maintain order on Hephaestus. To maintain order, and to maintain the secure flow of Clay ore to Earth, by any means necessary."

I signed on to organize a planetary defense and shipping lanes, Daniel thought, *not to be a dictator-for-hire.* This would lead to riots at a minimum. *At a minimum.* "Permission to speak freely?"

"Very well, Captain."

"Thank you. You mention 'any means.' I had already used an efficient and non-violent means, which had been working quite well to this point."

"True, Captain," Sydney said. "This is one reason why I need your experience. But in any case, that particular means is no longer available to you."

"In that case, martial law may be necessary." *If it would even hold*, Daniel thought. He had a few tens of thousands of personnel. Many operational personnel. Many of the combat troops were pilots—useless in enforcing such a state. Mostly the troops he could use were MPs—lacking credibility on Hephaestus after the *Hammer* incident.

"Yes, we have considered that this may be the most likely outcome. But not to worry. Officially the role of military governor will fall to me. You will only have the concrete job of keeping things in order. And should it come to this, I will expect reports from you on a daily basis."

H istorians in later years would assume that what happened next was a foregone conclusion, even as events played out back on Hephaestus. While the small Captain's Yacht took him back to Hephaestus, Daniel spoke to no one, and had chosen to avoid any of the news. Not NorthStar, not the *Hammer*, not any of the others.

The vessel moved through space, heading on its pre-programmed course. Daniel, though, no longer knew his destination. He moved from rationalizing to anger, to anxiety, and back again.

All the work I've done for 15 years, he thought, staring out the viewport at the black, *and none of it counts for anything*. Not the reviews from superiors. Not the special support from Neil. *Not even winning the fucking war*. Hell, in the Regular Navy, he could never even by flight-qualified to operate a fighter. *Even though* his sim scores were in the 92nd percentile. Hell, it had even taken a special dispensation from Neil just to *get him access* to a sim. Because he had the wrong ancestors.

And on Hephaestus: All the balancing, trading off, all the diplomacy… It all fell to shit, anyway. About the only thing that went right—that still would be right he hoped—were the morale improvements in the garrison force. Most of which, arguably, had come from Winstead's departure. Although Daniel had gone out of his way to treat everyone in his command with respect—not with the disdain in Sydney's treatment of him; the disdain reeking from the letter Winstead had left on his desk.

But, what would happen next? Certainly there would be a reaction when word of Sydney's orders hit Hephaestus. There were two possibilities. Most likely, there'd be protests and riots like the ones that got Winstead evicted. There was an outside chance of a more radical move.

He'd be charged with suppressing the riots and the protests. Which would alienate the local population; and also some of his troops.

On the other hand, there was an outside possibility that the colony—or, maybe, just the Gulch—would go so far as declare independence. Daniel had a mind, if they did, to go along with it. That scenario, at least, was clear. Sydney would probably order a blockade rather than an assault. A blockade could be broken. Conceptually easy—it would just take getting a call out to the other powers—but difficult in execution. With the blockade broken and Clay going from Hephaestus to Europe and Mars, the next step *then* would be invasion. And by that time, Europe and Mars, and maybe the Southern and Asian Blocks, too, would have vested interests in keeping the trade in Hephaestus Clay open.

What were his options otherwise? Resign his commission, become a privateer? Follow distasteful orders? Perhaps the only option he could think of: Give a comment to the *Hammer*, beg for calm. In the remaining hours, Daniel tried to draft a statement, for all the good it might do.

A committee was waiting for him, at the elevator dock, when he got back. Standing on the landing platform, in a semicircle: The Meres. Hamm. Franklin. Half the NewPort city Council. Also, Parker, with a selection of the junior officers and certain of the senior non-commissioned officers.

"We heard what happened," Parker said. "Everyone has."

"Is that what the welcoming committee is about?" Daniel asked.

"A small part," Franklin said. "What was done to you, and to Jack and Claire, has become a catalyst precipitating something that's been brewing here for a while now."

"Unless we've had a drought, precipitation can't be good," he said.

Franklin made a few strokes on her pad, and Daniel's own rang. He took it out of his pocket, and unfolded the screen to read better. "This will be published on the *Hammer* in about an hour," she said. "And then we'll have a live announcement to follow-up."

The story explained: NewPort and the Gulch and the InBot Syndicate had merged governments and formed a "Congress," which provisionally would also include representatives from three of the other smaller nearby colonies (they were en route, but had been involved by quantum link). Jack Mere had been elected President of the Congress; the former Speaker of the NewPort Council had been elected Vice President. And a formal statement had been promulgated.

"You didn't fail, sir," Parker said. "I know, having been here under Winstead. They'd—we'd have done this then, or soon after, without you're being here."

"He's right," Mere said. "Personally, I have watched you since just before you arrived, and I had been amazed by what you accomplished. The plain fact is you never had a chance, ultimately. You held things together as long as you did in part because you had Wallace's backing. Until someone on Earth got ruffled, and had Wallace yanked."

"The Kennedys," Daniel said.

"Presumably."

"Not presumably. Sydney as much as told me straight out. Over the logistics purchases."

Mere nodded. "I'd already heard," he said, "I got word right after you left. We voted on many things this past week," Mere said. "Not just this resolution. We also voted to offer command of planetary defense to you."

"What would make you think I might accept that commission?" he asked. "And, also, what would make you think that I would be the best choice, even if I did?"

Jack said, "You'd have already declared martial law, if you were on board with Sydney. That you didn't—that you've been out of touch for a week—said that you had a lot to think about. Just as we did. As for your qualifications? The one that matters most right now is our confidence; which you surely have."

We could really do this, he thought. No more half-measures. No more disrespect. And even if they were to lose, any settlement would have to include respect for the original charters.

"OK, then" he said. "Now here is the thing. If we are going to do this—if we're to pull this revolution off—here is what we have to do…"

Sea Change

Barely glancing at the mirror, Emily worked her straight brown hair up into a bun that fit neatly beneath her cap. She was looking more at the TV panel on the wall, where *yet another* Kirsten Davidson for President commercial ran.

This one featured a collection of people-on-the-street giving one-liners about their concerns. A girl in her twenties: "I think we can't be afraid to stand up to the Confederates, and Davidson would do that." Then a man—could be anywhere from 35 to 60—in a business suit: "They say they just want co-existence, but my father told me that at the tricentennial they promised not to secede again; you can't trust them; I think Davidson would stand up to them, and Danny Kane has already said that he wouldn't." Then the voice-over: "Kirsten Davidson: Keeping our borders safe; Standing up for United States Ideals. The President we need in 2112."

Whoever was in charge of Davidson's fundraising, Emily thought, was doing a bang-up job. You practically couldn't turn *anywhere* without coming across some sort of ad. Even if she still lagged in the polls.

On Emily's Plan of the Day: Briefing about the algae with the Bio/Biohaz team. Then a briefing with the Executive Vice President from Lake Algae Energy. Lunch in the Officer's Mess here on shore. And then a video debrief with Admiral Black. And no chance to get back to the *Grant*.

When she got to the conference room, an Ensign told her that her scientists wanted to see her at the lab.

When she got there, she found Lipton and DiNapoli—two reservist research scientists—staring at a huge dead fish half dissected on a lab table. The fish on the table was a giant—perhaps two meters long; half a meter in diameter, with a black stripe down the side.

"What do we have here?" she asked, from behind them before they had noticed that she'd entered the room. They both jumped; which made Emily smile just slightly.

"Captain!" Lipton said. "We, um, came across something interesting."

"I'd say so," she replied. "What is it?"

"We're not exactly sure yet," DiNapoli said. "We put out a few traps—took a few old fish cages; baited and weighted them. We came up with about five or six of these. By its shape, it should be a *Crossocheilus siamensis*; more commonly, a Siamese Algae Eater, usually an aquarium fish. Except that these are ten times bigger."

"We assumed these were genetically modified, so we ran a sequence," Lipton said. "But there's no IP marker on the 15th Chromosome."

Someone doesn't want it known who designed these things, Emily thought. It was an internationally adopted convention that any GM organism would carry its design information encoded in on the 15th chromosome. There should be an A-C sequence that could be decoded—A for 1, C for 0, in a 16-bit format; read the bases, and the name of whoever owned the patent would come up.

This would be the last step in a designer organism's genome. But Emily knew, from her undergraduate days, that even at the outset the organism engineer would have planted something else someplace else. The engineer doing the work would want to have some proof for claiming credit, even if the corporate or institutional bosses didn't. And the managers, usually, would not know about the second code.

Often particular companies or institutions had favorite places to put it. At MIT, her *alma mater*, tradition was that you'd put it someplace on the 28th chromosome. It might take a little library research, but it wouldn't be too hard to come up with a short list of likely sources and their favorite hiding places. "Check the literature," she said to the two scientists. "Find out who works with fish; then go through the sequence at the most likely chromosomes. And we need this as soon as possible. Three days ago would be optimum."

The buzz on her wrist had been a welcome interruption for Emily. The LAkE VP had already spent 45 minutes detailing, via slides, exactly how the missing algae could impact his company's earnings. The upshot was that he wanted the same thing she did—to find out what was going on and to reverse it. It didn't have to take 45 minutes—plus—to get to the point, and for her to tell him that there wasn't anything that the U.S. Navy could tell him yet, either. It was an effort of will to use the tools she'd acquired in her diplomatic training to feign interest.

The brief message she got on her wrist told her, though, that Lipton and DiNapoli might have found something. So she excused herself and returned to base.

They were waiting for her in her office.

"We have four characters," Lipton said, handing her his tablet. Four letters—RKUH.

"And something else," DiNapoli said. "These fish seem to have digestive tracts that process food very rapidly. And they have twin reproductive tracts so they must be reproducing *very* rapidly."

"Not a surprise, either of those two items," Emily said.

"We haven't gotten a lead on those four letters yet," Lipton said. "We're trying to match them up against every company and institution we can think of—we've got three military servers working on it."

"In what language?" Emily asked.

Lipton looked at DiNapoli, who looked back, and shrugged. "English," Lipton said, looking at her like she was nuts.

"It's German," she said. After four years at the former American Army Base School in Heidelberg, she knew what the letters meant: "It's Ruprecht Karl Universität Heidelberg—University of Heidelberg, in English."

The two scientists exchanged looks again. "So what do you want us to do about it now?" DiNapoli asked.

"Wait for orders," she said. "Dismissed." She checked the time as they left. Her debrief with Admiral Black was in less than an hour. She spent the time trying to get as much of a handle on what they'd already learned as she could. She had at least a rough outline of what she would report when her time ran out.

She turned on the holos, stood, and straightened her uniform. The image of her mentor, Admiral Black, in his Pentagon office, appeared. Emily saluted. The Admiral returned the salute, and asked her to sit.

119

The Admiral's hair had gone a little more white in the last two weeks, Emily thought. "Sir: We have caught an invasive, genetically-modified—"

Admiral Black cut her off with a wave of his hand. "I have a mission for you, Captain," he said.

"Sir?" she asked, confused.

"I need you to take the *Grant* to Buffalo, and to debrief Senator Winter at her district office there."

"Sir, yes, sir," she said, "but about what we've found…?"

"Please forward a report on what you've got so far," he said. "We may be able to take it from here, and even what you've got so far will be important for your meeting with the Senator. But, Emily, I am asking this of you in particular. I need someone I can trust with someone in Senator Winter's position."

Emily looked past the Admiral, out the window in her "side" of the meeting. Amy Winter, Senator from the state of West New York; ranking member of the Armed Services Committee. An important person. Still.

"Emily," the Admiral said.

She turned her full attention back to him.

"Do you know why I recommended you for the Lake Command?" he asked.

"May I speak freely?" she asked. He nodded. "I am a highly-qualified female officer," she said. "Too qualified to be passed over. So I am given one of the least consequential commands available."

"You have a BS in Organism Engineering, ROTC training, combat experience, and a Masters in Diplomacy. The Lakes are our energy center. And if you look at the map, you'll also see a great vulnerability opening this extremely sensitive area to the Confederacy."

"You mean the Mississippi? The river flows *away* from the lakes," she observed.

"It does. Which does not mean threats can't come upstream. There are other pieces of information you need to know. Please take a quick look at these—" he tapped a few strokes on his desktop tablet. An email appeared at Emily's side. Another slideshow with bullet-points.

First point: Gas emissions from the Confederacy indicated that they seemed to be burning less algae-oil, even though their orders to LAkE for oil hadn't fallen. Second point: Southern ports were receiving large shipments from Germany and China—likely solar panels and solar components.

"This is a pattern?" she asked.

120

Admiral Black nodded, "Naval Intelligence thinks so. Admiral Clark has been briefing the other Chiefs of Staff. The Navy is concerned that something very bad could happen in the very near future. Our mission is to see to it that the civilian leadership—all of it—is adequately informed; but without usurping their decision-making role. Which makes this an exceptionally delicate assignment."

B ecause Admiral Black had ordered her to take the *Grant* to Buffalo, instead of just flying, what could have been a one-day trip
(one-hour flight followed by an hour or two with the Senator, and
then another hour back) had become a week-long mission.

At 30 knots, it would take almost two days, up Lake Michigan, into
Lake Huron, through the canal and through Lake St. Claire, and finally to
the eastern side of Lake Eerie, and Buffalo.

She sat at the desk in her stateroom, looking over Lipton and DiNapoli's
latest reports.

She could feel the vibrations in the deckplates change frequency as the
ship moved out.

University of Heidelberg, she thought. She recognized the abbreviation
because she herself had spent three of her teen years there. Her father—a
nuclear engineer—had been stationed at what was then still the American
base there.

That was before Secession. After the New Confederacy left the Union,
what was left of the United States had withdrawn from the base. And that
had been 30+ years ago already.

Now, what was called the United States stretched from Vermont to
Maryland and the District of Columbia down the Eastern Seaboard;

the Great Lake states to Minnesota, and then Washington, Oregon, and California. And Hawaii. The rest was the New Confederacy.

The U.S. had fewer states but three times the population and ten times the economic output. *And a third of the will*, Emily thought. This time around, there had been no Lincoln. Only a President Gomez afraid of how a second Civil War would impact his chances at re-election, who chose to let the South go. (He was probably also figuring that he'd lost the South in his first campaign; letting them leave would alter the Electoral College in his favor. Except that he was wrong, and soundly voted out of office.)

There was a knock on the door. "Yes?" she asked.

"Colonel Stewart, Ma'am." The rich baritone of her Marine commander.

"Come in," she said, "have a seat."

The Colonel, close to 50 (but looking more like close to 30, except for the gray in his close-cropped afro) cut an impressive figure in his freshly-pressed fatigues. He sat down in the chair opposite the Captain's desk.

"Glad you're here," she said. "We have something of an unusual mission here. How familiar are you with politics?"

"I've been a political junkie since I was twelve," Stewart said. "Actually how I got interested in the Marines in the first place. Why do you ask now?"

Good question, she thought. She'd been his commanding officer for five years. They'd discussed music, food, baseball. And while you wouldn't want to discuss partisan politics, intellectual interests might have been in there somewhere. "I am to debrief a Senator from West New York in two days," she said. "And I've not the slightest about how to go about it. I mean, with the politics."

"Which of the two?"

"Amy Winters."

Stewart ran a hand across his face. "She's the ranking Republican member of the Armed Service Committee," he said. "Also, probably, the chair of the Republican caucus, but they don't make those positions public anymore, so that's conjecture."

"Yes," she said. "I believe that is why we've been ordered to Buffalo to brief her."

"That she insists on being briefed at her district office instead of in DC is a statement."

Emily already knew this—Admiral Black had as much as stated so. She knew that Winter was a pro-Southern Republican, and she'd read her web site. But the further intricacies were less clear. And Senator Winter had a

123

reputation: She had chewed up Navy briefers before.

"She holds a particularly delicate position," Stewart said. "Of the three parties, the Republicans have the smallest number of seats in Congress. The Democrats and Liberals usually coalesce on most issues, except where the Confederacy is concerned, where they can end up allying with the Republicans. And both the Liberals and Republicans are nervous that Davidson is gaining in the polls."

"Her rhetoric is just rhetoric," Emily said. "I can't see that there's any way she'd start a war if she gets in. I can't see anyone would take that seriously."

"Really?" Stewart asked. He took his phone off his wrist, tapped at the face, and set it on the desk. A hologram of Bull Clancy's stubbly jowls projected from it.

"Now those Commies in the North—in the *Union*—they claim all they want is co-existence. But if that's true, then what do you do with all the noise coming from that woman—what's her name—Davidson? By the way, is that a Christian name?

"I mean, they're sitting on an ocean of biofuel—what they call a 'lake,' and out of the goodness of their hearts, they let us buy a trickle. And then they make up stories about how there's not enough *real* oil left in the middle east or under the Gulf of Mexico—*our* territorial waters, by the way—and the price goes up.

"Are these the things you'd want to do to a neighbor you wanted to co-exist with? I don't think so. No, they're gearing up. This idea that they let us go in 2085? They knew they couldn't beat us then, and they were just buying time."

Stewart reached over and stopped the hologram, freezing it mid-diatribe.

"That's just Bull Clancy," Emily said. "He's a blow-hard. No one takes him seriously."

"No one in Chicago," Stewart said, "or New York or DC. But they take him very seriously in Atlanta and Houston. And in Buffalo and Pittsburgh, too."

When I first entered politics, that flag had 52 stars." Senator Amy Winters, grey hair pulled back in a bun, stood in front of the floor-to-ceiling window, her back to Emily, looking out at the Lake.

The Senator's district office took up three high floors of the old City Hall tower on Niagara Square. Her private office must have been 40 meters square, paneled in dark wood. Emily stood alone, attention-straight. The Colonel, and her XO, were left in waiting in the anteroom. Senator Winter had wanted to see her alone.

"You probably don't remember what that was like, a unified country," the Senator said.

"I was in my late teens when it happened, Ma'am," Emily said.

"It wouldn't have been the same for you, though. You're not really American, are you?"

"Yes, Ma'am, I am," Emily said. "My father was a Major in the Army Corps of Engineers; I was born on the U.S. tracking base that we had had in Greenland."

Winters turned around. "I hear some sort of accent—inflection, though."

Much of the time, Emily made some (small) effort to "normalize" her speech. Not this time, though. "My mother is British; I spent my early childhood in London, early teen years in Germany."

"And college?"

"Both undergraduate and graduate school were both in Boston, but several years apart. I was Navy ROTC; went to my first deployment after I earned my BS."

"In?" Winters asked. "And from where? I realize there aren't many universities in Boston." The Senator's mouth made an attempt at a smile.

"Organism Engineering. From MIT, Ma'am."

Winters stopped at that. "I see," she said. "Were you here when we split apart?"

"Yes, Ma'am. We were living in New York City by that time." Which was not entirely true; but it was a small fudge. Technically, they had moved to New York when secession became "official," which was already a few months after the first declaration.

"What did you think about it? You can speak freely."

No, I can't, Emily thought. Her training (and experience) in diplomatic communication told her this question was a rhetorical trap. Likely, almost anything she would say would wrong. In such a case, the best way to be wrong would be by sticking as close as possible to regulations—specifically, to the policy of deferring political opinions to the civilian leadership. "I believe I was too young to have a truly informed opinion, Ma'am."

That almost-smile returned to Winters' face. "And now?"

"I believe it is too late for an informed opinion to matter."

"You and I both know that that may not be the case," Winters said. "Especially if my distinguished colleague from Metro New York becomes President. You won't ask, but I'll tell you anyway, how I felt. I was a freshman Representative from a rural district near here. 'Conflicted' might be a pale approximation. Rending the nation rent my heart. But in some ways, my rural constituents and I could understand where the Confederates were coming from. And it broke my heart that we could not stay one nation, under a more tolerant government. But the Liberals and the Democrats in Washington wouldn't let that be." She smoothed her slacks with her hands, and then said, "Well. So much for that. Let's have a seat, shall we?" She sat in one of the armchairs arrayed in front of her desk, and motioned for Emily to take one of the others. "What have you got to show me?"

"Ma'am. As I am sure you are aware, there has been a precipitous decline in the bio-oil-producing algae in three of the Great Lakes. In the last three days, we have captured a small number of specimens of a fish, genetically-modified from a common algae-eater. This fish, however, is some two meters long, and has two separate reproductive tracts, meaning that it eats quite a lot, and reproduces exceptionally quickly."

As she spoke, she could see Winters' face express consternation.

"Any clue as to where these things came from?" she asked.

"Yes, Ma'am. Some early information. We were able to determine that the genetic modification had been done at the University of Heidelberg in Germany."

"Germany?"

"Yes, Ma'am. We do not yet know specifically by whom. Naval Intelligence and the CIA are at work on this presently."

"But there's no—is there any evidence at all that these came from Atlanta?"

So that was the basic question, Emily thought. Colonel Stewart had told her that certain Liberal web sites had reported that Winters was getting a good chunk of her campaign financing from out of the Confederacy. "No, Ma'am, there isn't," Emily said. "I imagine if there was, it would not be only me briefing you."

Winters smiled openly for the first time. "Yes, you have a *very* good point there, Captain. I like you. Personally, anyway—I still expect that our politics wouldn't match up well. But you seem like a straight-shooter. It was a real pleasure to meet you, Captain. Safe voyages." She held out her hand. Emily shook it, and then she was shown out.

Three months later, on the eve of the end of Election Season, Senator Winters had again requested a briefing. This time, in Washington, and in the context of hearings over a press leak.

The CIA had established tracked the custom genome from the algae-eating fish to the specific lab at Heidelberg that had made it, and from there established a link to a Southern aqua-culture company, whose CEO had links to President McCaskill, the Confederate Head-of-State.

And a news story had broken across the Web ten days before revealing this—crediting an anonymous source—revealing this information. This was a leak that helped in part to alter the complexion of the Presidential race.

Going in to the previous week, Davidson and Kane had been running in a virtual tie. Since the Secession, the Electoral College had an even number of electors, and projections were that this race could come to a tie, putting it into Congress. And in Congress, while the Democrats had a plurality, and often could legislate with help from the Liberals, together the Liberals and Republicans together would probably have elected Kane.

Since the story broke, though, Davidson had taken a 10-point lead, and was likely to win outright.

Consequently, the Republicans—even more so than the Liberals, even though Kane was running on the Liberal line—had become incensed, and ordered a (very rapid) investigation. Admiral Black was due to testify to Congress. At the same time, as the ranking Republican, Winters had requested another briefing from Emily.

The group under Emily's command had found the first evidence, and some suspicion was being cast on the Navy. Therefore, neither Admiral Black, nor the Navy Chief of Staff, nor the Secretary of the Navy wished to make things more difficult by opposing the request.

And so there she was, in Washington DC on the first Monday in November, at one of the Senate Office Buildings near the Capitol.

"Captain Marks, so good to see you again," the Senator greeted her when she was shown in to the private office. Winters grasped Emily's hand, at what Emily felt was a gratuitous show at warmth.

This office was a little less grand than the one in Buffalo. Still paneled in wood—blond this time—but the normal-sized window looked out on to an interior building courtyard. "I am exhausted," Winters said, as she settled into her desk chair. She motioned for Emily to take one of the seats opposite the desk. "I have just come from seven hours listening to testimony from your superior officer, among others." She looked at Emily, perhaps expecting a reaction.

Emily, though, did her best to project as neutral a reaction as possible.

"I am hoping that maybe you can give some additional context—off the record—to what I'm hearing on the record in the hearings," Winters said.

"I am not sure what I will be able to add, Ma'am. If you have specific questions, however, I will try to answer as best I can."

"Your group found the fish?" Winters asked.

"Yes, Ma'am. We found the first specimen, and in the last three months, have caught many, many more. The Pentagon has been using them to devise a way to limit their proliferation."

"How many people knew about it?"

"At the time at which I reported our initial finding, three people. The two military scientists who analyzed the specimen, and myself. I then reported the findings to my superior."

"When was that, Captain?"

"29 July."

"Three days before our first conversation," Winters noted. "Interesting timing."

In fact, it is, Emily thought to herself.

"I know that intellectuals and academics have not been fond of the Confederacy," Winters said. "There have been decades of protests at university campuses."

There had been protests since Secession, Emily thought. But the academics angry with the Confederacy often tended to be the Liberal constituency—who also typically opposed military action.

"Could your scientists have been the source of the leak?" Winters asked.

Emily had worked with DiNapoli and Lipton for five years. True, they were reservists and not regular Navy. But, still, they took their duties seriously. And neither of them were foolish enough to risk their careers on a leak. Plus, despite Winters' insinuation, neither of them had any motive. Especially not when balanced against the negative consequences if caught. "Extraordinarily unlikely," she said, finally.

"Someone in the Pentagon, at the Navy Department?"

"I would be very surprised if that was to be the case," Emily said. "Although I have no personal knowledge."

Winters stroked her chin, looking Emily up and down. Then she leaned back in her chair and crossed her legs. "So, let me ask you this, informally. And as an intelligent woman, not as a Navy Captain. If you could speculate, then, where do *you* think the leak came from?"

Emily actually hadn't had time to speculate about that. On the most basic level, really, she didn't care. But she, and Admiral Black, had expected that this sort of question might come. Not unlike the hypotheticals directed at the Admiral himself during testimony. Admiral Black had to wave them off; but Emily, here, wasn't under oath, and the Senator would probably not tolerate evasion in this context. So she had chosen to consult Colonel Stewart's political expertise. And she repeated—paraphrased—what he'd said to her.

"It seems to me that the motive was political; to influence the outcome of the election," she said.

"Not to provoke a war?" Winters asked.

Emily shook her head. "If the idea was to influence the election, then the presumption would be that they couldn't get a war resolution through Congress anyway."

"That's sure as Hell true," Winters said. "No unproven allegations would get us to vote for a war."

"So if it's about the election, then you'd have to look at people with access the information, and with a motive, and with press contacts. So the best place to look would probably be the staff of certain Democratic Senators. Particularly the Chair of the Armed Services Committee. Probably a mid-level staffer. Or consultant."

Winters stroked her chin again. "You've given me a few things to think about, Captain," she said. "Thank you again for coming in."

And with that, Emily was shown out.

By the time Emily got off of Capital Hill, it was mid-evening; polls would start closing in Massachusetts and New Jersey soon; a little later in New York and Pennsylvania. She hadn't any contacts who would be free tonight, and she didn't relish the thought of watching the election returns alone in a hotel room. So she took a cab across M Street to Georgetown. She was staying in a hotel in Rosslyn (convenient to both the Pentagon and Capitol Hill), and getting back would be just a short trip across Key Bridge.

She walked the few blocks west of Wisconsin Avenue to the small park where Key Bridge intersected M Street, and looked out across the Potomac. The towers in Arlington, in the State of Northern Virginia, reached skyward. Unlike the stunted-by-law low blocks of the District. Reminded her of Heidelberg (without the valley-defining hills), or even London. Although the Potomac was significantly wider here than either the Thames or the Neckar.

She remembered—she was standing in front of the monkey at the Alter Brucker on the Alt Stadt side, looking up at the Philosopher's Walk on the other side of the river. She was 14 in 2082, and she had already taken to walking out and across the Alter Brucker, and strolling up the mountain path. (*If it was good enough for Twain and Maugham*, she thought, *it would be good enough for me*.) That day, she'd been slow, spending extra time people-watching by the University and past the old church, and window-shopping the kitschy souvenirs on Hauptstrasse. To her left, the sun was just starting to head into the river, and she was considering turning back for home when her Watch went off. A text from her father, who was back at home, at what had been the American army base five minutes earlier. It said, "Come home now. South seceding."

She'd raced home, and huddled with her mother while her father attended the emergency briefing. There would be, it turned out, no war. And, probably, no more American bases overseas (and what did it mean, now, to be "American"?) Those from seceding states were given the opportunity to go home or join the Union. Most would stay in the Union, if their families back home could be evacuated north. And the Marks'? They packed up and headed for New York City—it would be the first time Emily—American citizen by birth—would live in North America full time. Dad got an engineering job with the Port Authority; Mom found a tenure-track spot at the City University. Emily breezed through Bronx Science; then to MIT and Navy ROTC…

She shook herself from her reverie. The sun had gone down—to her right, this time. Polls were closing. With modern Web voting, results would be instantly tabulated and reported quickly. Hungry, and in no mood to watch the returns in a barren hotel room, she turned back toward M Street, and strolled east down the main drag until she found what looked to be a hospitable enough bar.

She slid onto a stool, and ordered a burger and fries and beer. The bar was dimly lit, most of the light coming from 3D projectors. Toward one end, where they had a stage, they also had a small Holo-Plasma box (like the ones at the arena movies, only this one was, maybe, 40 inches across).

In the bar, a cross-section of young DC types. Late 20s through early 50s, various degrees of post-work, semi-loosened office wear. Obviously, like her, interested in the results, and wanting to be in public. Not unlike watching the World Series in a bar instead of at home. Some of them, on seeing her uniform, said, "Thank you," or something similar, as they passed by and met up with their friends. A few—Liberal staffers or lobbyists, she guessed—gave her condescending looks instead.

She was about half way through a pumpkin pie with whipped cream when the newscaster broke in with results. The entire bar went silent. Results were in from the Northeast: The seaboard from Vermont to Metro New York through Delaware: Davidson. Western New York, Maryland, Northern Virginia: Kane. In another hour, the results were clear: Illinois, Wisconsin, Oregon, Washington, California: All for Davidson. Shortly thereafter, Danny Kane appeared on a stage in a hotel ballroom in Madison, Wisconsin, to concede the race and congratulate Kristen Davidson.

Then the anchorperson announced that President-Elect Davidson, in a similar hotel ballroom in New York City, was getting ready to make her statement.

But before they could cut to her, another announcement broke in: Jackson McCaskill, the Confederate President, was *himself* addressing the Confederacy. They cut to him. Pale, jowly face, gray rapidly thinning hair, greased-back hair. Stars and Bars in the background. He said:

"Confederate friends. What many of us feared has now happened."

As he spoke, the network was running a crawl beneath his talking head. The first one said, "McCaskill is the second Confederate President, elected in 2090. (The Confederacy has no Presidential term limits.) Prior to that he was the most popular vidblogger in the South."

McCaskill continued: "The fascists in the North have voted in that Jew, Davidson."

The commentary from the crawl: "President-Elect Davidson is a practicing Unitarian. (She may have Jewish ancestry.)"

McCaskill went on. "We've all heard the rhetoric that's come out of Davidson. But we here have not been sitting idle. You know that this Administration has taken steps to increase the use of our own energy sources. So we don't have to buy the green sludge from the North. We've increased solar power. We have again begun drilling for good, old fashioned petroleum from our territorial waters in the Gulf of Mexico. You have also probably heard rumors from the Northern so-called press about an attack on their sludge.

"I can tell you, my Confederate friends, that those rumors are in fact true. And we are responsible. And we can promise our Northern friends more of the same if their new President goes down the path she's promised. We suggest she change her mind. Good night. And God bless the Confederate States of America."

The news anchor came back on. "What we've seen here is a statement by President McCaskill of the Confederacy... Wait, I'm getting word that President-Elect Davidson is ready to make a statement."

The scene changed to what looked like an enormous hotel ballroom. The crawl said, "Davidson HQ: Midtown Manhattan, Metro New York."

Davidson, straight plain brown shoulder-length hair, distinguished brown pantsuit, was holding an earpiece to her head with one hand, and gesturing at some aides with the other. When she realized the feed was on, she turned and assumed the podium.

"My fellow Americans, good evening. I think we have all just heard the statement from President McCaskill, so I will take the liberty of skipping the remarks I'd had prepared for tonight. I do want to briefly thank my campaign staff, Geoff Prince, my campaign manager, Zack Cohen, my Communications Director, and everyone else. You deserve more than I can say here now. I also wish to briefly salute Daniel Kane for his spirited and professionally-run campaign. He was nearly the one to be making this statement tonight.

"I made contact with President Chiu, and we both had a conference call with the Speaker of the House and the Senate Plurality Leader as soon as the intent of President McCaskill's statement became clear. I have asked if they would convene a joint session of Congress tomorrow morning. Many critical issues must be addressed, and urgently.

"Tonight, I am only the President-Elect and have no formal executive power. I am, however, still the sitting Senior Senator from the State of Metro New York. I will use what privileges I have in that position under the Constitution to do what I can until I can be inaugurated.

"This will not be an easy transition. Every American may be called on in this crisis. I will end tonight with the words of Benjamin Franklin, who said, in a not dissimilar crisis, that we must all hang together or assuredly we shall all hang separately. Good night. And may God bless us all."

During the speech, Emily's Watch rang. Recognizing the incoming IP, she reached in her pocked for her own earpiece. She answered. "Marks, go."

"Black here," the Admiral said. "Captain, you are ordered to appear at the Office of the Chief of Staff of the Navy in the Pentagon at 07:00 tomorrow. There will be a briefing. Immediately following, you will accompany us to the Congressional join session, where we may be called on to give expert testimony."

"Sir, yes, sir," she replied.

"Also, I am sending you materials for this briefing. Familiarize yourself with this material prior to the briefing. Over and out."

Emily put the earpiece away and stood up. She paid her tab and turned to go. She would have to catch a cab to get back to the hotel as efficiently as possible (*So much for a pleasant walk across the bridge,* she thought.) As she turned for the door, she could feel every pair of eyes falling on her. She turned back for a moment. One of them said, "We're all counting on all of you."

The group from the Navy sat toward the front of the Congressional Gallery, near groups from the other service arms (Coast Guard on one side, Air Force on the other) and included Admiral Black, the Navy Chief of Staff, Chief of Naval Intelligence, and the Marine Corps Commandant.

The Senators and Representatives filed in. The Sergeant at Arms announced the President. President Chiu came into the chamber, took the podium, and said, "Mr. Speaker, Madame Plurality Leader; I request that we hear from the President-Elect."

"The Chair recognizes the Senator from Metro New York."

Davidson rose, and walked to the well. At the microphone, she said, "I would like to cede my time to the Senior Senator from West New York."

The chamber—even (especially?) the Gallery—erupted. No one expected this. They were expecting Davidson to speak—perhaps give an impassioned and eloquent speech. Ask for a decision from Congress. They didn't expect her to cede her time to the leader of the party that didn't field a Presidential candidate.

Nonetheless, Senator Winters rose and walked to the well. She said, "Fellow Senators. Americans watching at work or at home. Representatives.

"I am reminded today that there was a time when the President-Elect and I were both Representatives from the former State of New York. I was in my eighth term when Senator Davidson began her Freshman year in 2084. While I found my new colleague very smart, and very prepared, she and I agreed on hardly anything. Except maybe where to go for lunch."

That inspired a brief wave of laughing.

Winters continued. "Rissoli's in Union Station, by the way. Anyway. And everyone knows what happened the following year. She and I did not agree on what the proper response should have been.

"My district—back when I was a Representative—is a rural district in West New York, just beyond the outskirts of Buffalo. In many ways, the feelings there are not dissimilar from the feelings in the South. My constituents and I at the time, while not agreeing with secession, could understand and sympathize with the frustrations in the south. We felt: Live and let live. And that has been the approach of the United States ever since. And I will not pretend that Republicans from rural areas have, since, worked to keep that status quo as it has been since 2085."

She paused, and looked down at her Watch, as though she was looking at her notes. Emily thought, rather, it was nothing more than a dramatic effect.

Winters continued. "The statement last night from McCaskill, though, has caused something of a sea change. For me, personally, and for many in the Republican Caucus. For me in particular, the Rebel assault on the Great Lakes—I remind everyone that Buffalo is a port city on Lake Eerie—and on one of our major energy sources in the genetically modified algae we've been growing in the Lakes—has struck more than just a nerve."

When Winters used the word, "Rebel," a wave of unrest propagated through the room. Rebel was a loaded word; usually, only Democrats—and only angry Democrats—referred to the Confederacy as "rebels," recalling as it did the 19th Century Civil War.

"They have committed an unprovoked act of war against the United States. They may claim it is not unprovoked, but the fact that they may not like the stances of a given candidate is *not* a provocation. It is an attack that, I feel, cannot go unanswered.

"Our caucus has had brief conversations over night, and we have not yet come to consensus. I have also spoken to the President-Elect over night, as she reached out to me. I know she will be putting forth a difficult resolution today. And I urge everyone in this body—especially my own caucus, but also the Liberals—to give it your support. Thank you, and my thanks to Senator—President-Elect—Davidson for ceding me her time."

Winters returned to her seat.

The Plurality Leader (Senator from Minnesota) turned to Davidson. "Senator, you have one minute remaining on your time."

Davidson rose, walked to the well, and said, "My friend from West New York is right. This cannot go unanswered. I move for—whatever you want to call it, whatever can pass: Declaration of war; authorization of force; proclamation of self-defense. It doesn't matter what we call it." She returned to her seat.

Emily looked from the Floor to the Podium, where President Chiu had been watching the proceedings. High cheekbones that had grown lined, under white, straight hair. Normally with the expression of supreme confidence of someone who'd gone through 75 years without major setbacks. Now, his features fell, and he slumped back. Probably realizing, Emily thought, that he was about to take (temporary) command of a war he didn't want.

And with that, she realized that, rather than a backwater, her command was likely to become a major front in that war.

The Unlit Unknown

In the triple cities, snow season started in mid-October. The first
flurries had come before Halloween, and had stopped by every-
day—sometimes only for fifteen minutes, but still—since. They called
Binghamton-Johnson City-Endicott area the "southern tier." Hardly anything *southern* about the climate, Tammy Finklestein thought, gathering
her Thinsulate raincoat around her.

She fumbled for the car keys, breath condensing in a cloud around her.
The 11-year-old crossover (the procurement of which had been arranged
by Seth—some parting gift, she thought) had a thin film of ice. Something
else new, she thought. A decade living in Boston, and now this. Not only
was the weather *worse* than in New England, but there was no T—no public
anything of any note, especially outside of the SUNY campus. Not that
Binghamton University was such a joy. Sure, the library was OK (and thanks
to the Internet, more than serviceable) and the computer services ran well
(thanks to the Engineering school), but the *food*... Better not to think about
it, she thought.

At least there wasn't so much rush hour traffic, so getting to her office in
the Physics department didn't take long, so she had some extra time before
her first class: Teaching remedial physics to basketball players.

139

The blonde woman in the pink dress cut Tammy off as she tried to sneak out of the post-service coffee hour.

The service had been pleasant—the choir good, the keyboard player competent. The pastor—a tall man with a thin nose and graying temples—gave a sermon that bordered on the intellectual. Maybe this was the most promising of the places she'd been?

"Hello," the woman said. "Haven't seen you around here before. I'm Sylvie—I'm the head of the Greeter's Committee. And you are?"

Tammy decided that polite and curt answers might be the quickest way out. So, she said, "Tammy Finkelstein. Nice to meet you. But I'm in a little bit of a rush."

"Finkelstein?" Sylvie said. "Wouldn't that be, you know, a *Jewish* name?"

"My father was Jewish, my mother was Church of Christ."

"Oh, I see. And how did you come to be in our little church today?"

Little church? Tammy thought. The place on Main Street wasn't a mega-church but it was hardly small. And the service had had maybe 200 people. Impressive, actually, that this Sylvie woman would notice a newcomer in that crowd.

"I'm new in town. I've been looking around. Going across the city map, trying different churches," Tammy said.

"New in town? Well, welcome. Hope the weather doesn't depress you. You know, we have cloudier weather than *Seattle,* if you can believe that! But what brings you to the Triple Cities?"

"I'm at SUNY," Tammy said. "I just started this semester."

"SUNY—really?" Sylvie said. "Don't get too many of you types in church. I can tell you. Except some of the staff. Are you staff?"

"Faculty," Tammy said. "Tenure track. Or so they tell me."

"Which department?"

"Physics."

Sylvie's eyes seemed to triple in size. "Well, you *are* an odd one. Don't get *any* scientists from the university coming in here. Well—we used to get some of the engineers from the aerospace companies. That was before that horrible Clinton shut them all down!"

Tammy held her tongue. She knew full well it was Bush—the first one, not the son—who'd downsized the military. And she also knew, if she didn't want to get embroiled in this conversation to correct her. "I know—the area's been pretty hard-hit," she said. "Look—I'm sorry—but I really do have to go. It was nice to meet you, Sylvie."

"Nice to meet you too, sweetie," Sylvie said. "Look, I'll let you go, but I want you to know that we're having a gathering for prospective members—some on the younger side, like you," she leaned a little closer and whispered, "and some of them male and single and *cute.*" She backed away again. "It'd be lovely if you could come. If you'll just leave your email or give me your number?"

What's to lose? Tammy thought. She gave Sylvie her email address, got hers in return, and walked out into the freeze-dried Binghamton night.

Tammy saw that Seth was on Facebook. She clicked on him; accepting the pang that came with seeing the tag, "Single." It hadn't been that long ago.

But he was chatting. A chat box popped up: "Hey Tammy Busy tonight?"

She stared at the box for an 15 seconds—an Internet eternity. Finally she typed, "Grading remedial pre-calc papers. Came all the way out here for this."

"What about the promises?" he wrote back.

The promises. Allen had promised her lab time; teaching of graduate classes; and a tenure track. So far, only the last one still seemed viable. Probably only because it'd been in the contract. And even so Tammy doubted, the way things were going, that anything would come of it. As it stood, her value to the department was that she was a female physicist, and that she was stuck. "Not worth the silicon they were transmitted on," she tapped back.

"Change the terms of the equation," he wrote back. "Publish."

Easy for him to say, she thought. Seth worked on quantum computation—a small, but hot and growing field. And it just so happened that his interests coincided with what the top journals wanted to publish. Not so Tammy's research. She published, sure. But the places that were interested in the mix of quantum mechanics, psychiatry, and philosophy—and nothing practical—tended to have Impact Factors south of 1.

"I publish," she said. "I may do a book."

"Publish the visual cortex slit paper."

The visual cortex slit paper... Two years ago, when they were dating, Tammy had helped Seth out with an experiment involving visual cortex iimplants in blind people and the double-slit experiment. If it had been worth publishing, Seth would have done it by now. "Then why haven't you published it?" she wrote.

"Not central enough—not enough time," he said. "You should. I'll email the files. Be lead author. But include me." And then he logged off from Facebook. And the files arrived in her inbox about a minute later.

She looked at the email and the attachments in her inbox. He'd sent it with the subject line: "For PRL". PRL was *Physical Review Letters*—probably the fourth most prestigious journal to be published in. After *Science*, *Nature*, and *Nature Physics*. Actually—scratch that. PRL might be better than *Nature Physics*.

The problem with publishing the paper—other than the issues around accepting credit as a gift from Seth—was the selling out. Giving in to Allen's prejudices about what kind of research was valuable. The thought stuck.

On the other hand. It was actual research she had actually done. Just not written up and submitted. What would be the harm? In just throwing it out there?

Fred Allen had a bookcase in his chairperson's office filled with his books. Not books he owned—books he'd written, or to which he'd contributed chapters. And he'd arranged the bookcase so that anyone sitting in his office guest chairs couldn't help but see them. The ones he'd written propped up, face-out. The others, spined. All in mint condition—even the paperbacks. Because, of course, he'd never *open* them. Not when he had all of them on his iPad.

Allen sat straight, graying hair parted on the side. A vial of glasses cleaner still sat on the corner of his desk, even though he'd had lasik the year before. He said, "I understand your frustration, Dr. Finkelstein. In fact, I've never ever supported the University getting involved in big time basketball. Hell—I didn't even like when they changed the University's *name*."

Schools re-brand all the time, Tammy thought. She'd realized that at some point, the place had started calling itself "Binghamton University" (with a logo clipped straight from Boston University's—the other "BU") instead of SUNY-Binghamton. So had Tufts—her undergraduate alma mater—re-done its logo a few years ago. No one there seemed at all perturbed. But she supposed that this—like everything else—was different here.

Allen continued. "But we do have to at least make the attempt, right?

143

And you're the new person here—low person on the totem pole, if you will. So I'm sorry to tell you it falls to you." He spoke in that kind of voice meant to give the impression that he cared; that he sympathized. Most people, Tammy thought, would probably buy into it. Looking over at the books (and having done a Web of Knowledge search on the whole department while she was applying for the spot), she knew Allen's type. Not the best researcher—not himself the leading light. But he knew everyone. And he could get them to do things for him. Which was how his name had been attached—not as lead author, but still attached—on some of the most important papers of the last ten years in optics and opto-electronics.

"So perhaps I can at least look forward to someone else taking this on next semester?"

"The course offerings for next semester were already set—they have to be put into the database already," he said. "So I'm afraid not."

"Next year?"

"Well, that depends on you," he said. "For example, do you have any papers out under consideration that might be accepted someplace interesting soon?"

She didn't. That had been part of her problem at MIT, too. Her work in quantum consciousness was a long-term endeavor. The hard problem of consciousness wasn't going to be solved—probably not by her, probably not alone, and definitely not in a 10-page journal paper. And publishing pablum and mathematically clever guesses appalled her.

"Well. We hired you because, even with a thin publication record, other aspects of your CV were appealing. And we felt you would be a good fit—especially for teaching. And if you chose to not publish as much as the others in the department, then it would be logical for me to keep you in that primary teaching role."

Tammy said nothing. She'd been put in check. Maybe, she thought wryly, she should have checked on Allen's reputation in chess.

"If there's nothing else?" Allen said.

"Not at this point," she replied.

"Well, then. Thank you for stopping by, Dr. Finkelestein. Best of luck—and remember, my door is open."

Tammy walked out into the mid-November afternoon flurries. Not too late for lunch, she thought, but probably too late to go off-campus, meaning she'd be stuck eating the sub-standard campus fare.

Tammy ran along the Chenango River, bundled in layers against the southern tier freeze. She could see right across the river, toward Vestal on the southern bank. Narrow river, she thought, that didn't compare to the Charles. She thought back—running through Cambridge on the west bank of the Charles, the Prudential and Hancock towers rising from the Back Bay.

This river had no such cityscape. A few buildings in Binghamton; and then shopping plazas. As far as they eye could see. A few blocks of a downtown. And then the Oakdale Mall. And Wegmans. Everyone, eventually, went to Wegmans. And while the rivers themselves— Binghamton was plopped down at the junction where the Chenango met the Susquehanna—were pretty, there wasn't much going on in the cities. And the path along the river was much less crowded (for running) than the paths along the Charles. Except for the cars coming down the Vestal Parkway.

S ylvie had called it a "gathering." Truer words were never spoken, as everyone there was gathering around Tammy. Come to stare at the church-shopping physicist, she thought.

"Actually, I was convinced by quantum mechanics," Tammy said. "Because, you know about the indeterminacy issue—the Schroedinger's Cat thing—and you end up with two choices. Either a new universe is born at every quantum probability junction, or there's *something* 'observing' everything. And I found that the latter was simpler than the former, and I used Occam's razor."

And the other newbies just stared, eyes a little blank.

"Is that actually a scientific argument for God, I hear?" Sylvie drawled.

"No, it isn't," Tammy said. "It's a philosophical one that has the effect of being *consistent* with science. It's not the same thing."

"I see," Sylvie said.

"Can you make a scientific case for God?" A question from a large 40-something man, between bites of coffee cake.

"No," Tammy said.

"See—she's no different than the rest of those commies in Vestal," he said.

"I can make an argument as to why that's an irrelevant question, instead," Tammy said. "It goes like this. Science believes that the universe—as we observe it—started at the Big Bang about 14 billion years ago."

"Lies!" someone in the back said. "6,000 years ago!"

Tammy rubbed her forehead.

Sylvie said, "Hey—Roxanne—she's talking about God, not *Genesis*. Let's hear what she has to say!"

"Thanks, Sylvie," Tammy said, relieved someone stood up for her. Sort of. "Anyway. Big Bang. Right. So there's a starting point, when time started. Now, if you're talking about a *Creator*, then, by definition, you're talking about a consciousness that existed *before* the universe." The next part was the tricky part—the epiphany she'd had a few years before—the fun part. "Now, we know—or science or physics knows—from Einstein's General Relativity—that space and time are the same thing—space-time. So if space and time are one, and a Creator existed before the universe—outside the universe in time, then, *ipso facto*, this Creator *also* exists outside the universe in *space* as well. And empirical science has no way of observing what's beyond our universe. Which means, by definition, science can't say anything about God one way or another." She paused.

"Well, that's a *mouthful*," Sylvie said. "Let me get you—well, I was going to offer you some more *coffee*, but I think you've had about enough!" She smiled widely. "How on *Earth* did you think of all that?"

Tammy returned the smile. "I'd had a thought," she said, "I was working on a really annoying piece of math for my dissertation. And dealing with physical constants and how everything seemed set up for us. And the thought hit me that this universe, as it exists, would look the same to empirical science whether it *was* created or just happened."

Minister Shure stopped her on her way out to the street. "Interesting sermon—of a sort—there. I could overhear it from the other side of the room." He smile, corners of his eyes crinkling, amplifying the nascent wrinkles there. "So interesting—I wonder if you've preached science to us, could you preach the Word to the scientists?"

She stared at him, trying to keep her expression neutral. Not only were most scientists skeptics by nature (and training), and not only were most of them atheists, but also independent thinkers. Someone trying to convince them of something that's not in the math? Forget about it. What she said was, "To be honest, Reverend, I'm not yet sure myself that this is the place for *me*. And to try to convince someone else when I'm not myself convinced, I think..."

He waved his hand. "I understand, Professor. It was just a thought. And I do hope you decide this is the place for you."

"Thank you," she said. "And thank you for the compliment."

Tammy sat in the dark—illuminated only by the backlit glow from her LCD screens. Huddled in a sweatshirt against the late winter cold. Lazily paging through her email, she came across the files Seth had sent.

There'd reason—other than the lack of interest—that neither of them had written a paper about that work. She remembered the fight they'd had the last time they'd talked about it.

"I can't put my name on something applied," she said, "it'll dilute my CV."

"How can a publication credit be bad?" Seth had replied. "It's clear that it' snot your main focus. And I think we could get this into an APS journal—maybe even PRL. How could that hurt?"

"I only did this as a favor for you," she said. "It'll look like I don't take my main work seriously."

"That's ridiculous. It'll look like you have broader interests. That you're more versatile. More eclectic."

"And is it reasonable to expect one person to work in quantum information, and to work in philosophy, and also have a connection to neuroscience? Because that's what working on the hard consciousness problem means. And to toss in an *applied* paper? It would strain credulity." And even as she was saying it, she could tell—if it wasn't the words, it was they way she'd said them.

"An *applied* paper?" he mimicked. "So—what? Applied physics is only a hair's-breadth from engineering, and engineering is worthless? Is that it?"

"I didn't mean that," she said.

"No, you certainly did mean it," he said. "You're only regretting that it came out that way. You don't think the work in this lab is worth anything."

"You know that isn't true," she said. Anticipating the coming lecture about the laser, and about ultrasound, and about semiconductors and computers. About how communications research found the Microwave Background. It would be the fiftieth time, by her count, she'd heard it.

"OK, fine. I've convinced you. Now you think the work in this lab is worth a little."

"Sure it's worth something. Like airplanes and cars and computers are *worth* something. But its not the big questions. It's like Einstein in the patent office—do you think he wanted to *stay* there?"

"You're incredible," he said. "If you think that what I do is worthless, then you have to think that I'm worthless."

And that was the beginning of the end. She said she didn't think he was worthless, but wasting his abilities. He took more offense at that. And within the week, that was that.

That she'd belittled the Applied Lab got out; and the Applied Lab brought in a lot of money. So, naturally, a spotlight landed on her *own* recent publication list, which was sparse.

And that was how she landed in Binghamton. Where she was faced, again, with the same problem, with the same paper.

In that one moment, she saw it all—the entire pattern, the spirals and echoes, the replicating patterns, the fractal of it. The church, the humanities departments, the sciences—all of it, all the same.

The orthodoxy wasn't about *truth*, it was about power; about social control; about social status. It was the elementary school playground all over again—all about who had cooties and who was cool. And the ideas—the philosophies and doctrines themselves? Just the means to an end, not ends in themselves like Tammy had always thought.

At the church, it was still the same people—the athletes, the pretty girls—still at the top. In the philosophy and literature departments, the hipsters—the smokers, the heirs of the greasers, still in their own way rebelling against the athletes and the pretty girls. And in the sciences, the smart kids, the former mis-fits, often—cast out from the mainstream, replicating the same structures.

She'd been guilty of it, too—the comments she'd made—the *thoughts she'd had*—about Seth's work. About how theoretical physics—the "Big Questions" as she'd aggrandized it—were far more important than the work of making people's lives better.

Had she been doing it for the same reasons? Her work was "higher," so she was more important? Maybe not more important than Seth per se, but more important than applied physicists and engineers? Who saw themselves as more important than the humanities departments? (Math is hard, they say, and the Leisure Arts like writing are easy. But, she wondered, if writing is so much easier than math, then why are so many scientists so bad at it?)

On the other hand, there was the vision—the bad dream—you get caught up in the day-to-day, chasing the wrong things. And one day you find yourself ten years down the line, and the things you'd thought you'd have done? Even further away.

This was the core of Tammy's work—the "Hard Question" of consciousness—how did particles and chemicals, electromagnetism, and quantum mechanics form human subjective experience? Why *is* there human subjective experience when, by all rights, there *shouldn't* be? Among other things, her working theoretical basis put her at odds with information theory, as practiced and understood by the theoretical physics community. Because she was arguing against—as far as consciousness—and biology and creativity were concerned—the answer to the Black Hole Information Paradox developed by t'Hooft and Susskind. And t'Hooft had a Nobel to his name...

The idea was that, like matter and energy, the universe conserves information—information is neither created nor destroyed. And objects absorbed by black holes don't disappear—their information doesn't vanish—but gets spread out and "projected" on the event horizon. Related to that—information includes the *arrangements* of particles, from the quantum to the meso to the macro scale. And if information can't be destroyed, then any particular arrangement of particles—any, for example, crystal lattice or partially-ordered material like a glass—can be re-created and re-constructed—unscrambled, as they call it—from any starting point.

Yet there are arrangements of particles in non-random yet arbitrary patterns that have meaning—value—only to a consciousness that can de-code them—for example the arrangement of words on a page. Taken statistically, you have a certain quantity of ink molecules applied to a polymer-fiber matrix. The proportion of ink to polymer can be computed. The distribution of ink on the paper surface can be found to be relatively even, for example. Yet the *specific* distribution ink—formed into letters, formed from letters into words, sentences, paragraphs—statistically and chemically—blindly—show nothing. However, those patterns have *great* meaning to a human consciousness that can read. The same with sound waves and speech. Or music.

If we assume there is nothing particularly special about the molecular arrangement on the paper, then we'd have to hypothesize that the key is in the brain—or more properly, the consciousness—of the person reading.

How does a consciousness derive value from an arbitrary pattern? If we knew that... she thought.

And what about the Conservation of Information? That all movements of particles can be reconstructed, and that information is neither created nor destroyed?

Well, she thought, that didn't work, either. At least not at the *particular* level, even if does work on the statistical level. Why? Chaos and nonlinear dynamics. Without a record—or a key—if you can't predict with specificity where a macro-particle will *go*, then you can't reconstruct where it's been. And the particular arrangements *matter*. To consciousnesses, at least. *Hamlet*, after all, is *not* a random arrangement of ink, or sounds, pounded out by a thousand monkeys at a thousand typewriters. You know what it *isn't*, she thought. But that doesn't mean we know what it is.

The night before graduating, she tried to imagine it. Lack of consciousness. Death.

Probably, it was the major life-change. She hadn't been accepted yet to a graduate program—a screw-up with the Registrar not sending her the transcripts she ordered—and she didn't know what would come next after four years of living in academia.

And it was grandpa's yahrtzeit. She lit the candle, set out her robe, and tried to go to sleep.

And she lay there in bed, eyes wide open, staring in the dark. Was this what it was? She thought. Just darkness? No—less than that. No internal monologue. No sense of muted nighttime sounds. No memories. No sensation. Nothing. And if the entire universe in a way only existed in her perceptions of it, then wasn't death the end of the universe, in any way that matters to the individual? And if that's the case, then, does anything—anything at all—matter?

What will it be like to die? Is it even possible, in a real way? Maybe time just freezes at the last moment. Maybe you just cycle back again? Maybe you just exist in that last moment? Maybe you can't even think about what the end of consciousness is without knowing what consciousness itself is.

153

She'd wondered about death for as long as she could remember—but wrestling with it before was a passing shadow—ten minutes here, fifteen there. This time, it would not let go. Even in the brilliant May sunshine and family celebrations of her graduation. In books, in movies, death had always been described as a going dark—the fading of the light. But even there, there's still a "you" to perceive darkness. This she could grasp. But the other—absolute end—lay beyond, and terrified.

She spent the following days at the New York Public Library, scouring the catalogue and the Internet for anything—anything at all about consciousness—she could hang a shred of hope on. She came across David Chalmers, and Roger Penrose. And by the time the MIT grad school acceptance letter finally came, she'd picked her specialty.

Minister Shure stood at the lectern, rimless glasses slipping down his nose. He'd keep pushing it up with his finger as he read his sermon from the iPad on the lectern. He'd chosen to talk about the poor. About how the exhortation to care for the orphan, the widow, and the stranger applied to society as a whole, not just private charity; not just to the good works the congregation did.

As he spoke, Tammy could see the congregation—especially Sylvia—shifting in their chairs. Her husband folded his arms across his chest.

After, at the coffee hour. Cliques congealed, orbiting away from the minister. Whispering. Tammy hung back, watching. Guessing that the globs of churchmembers were whispering about him, and nothing else. This was a conservative place—and while Shure hadn't advocated any specific politics, the implication—support for the welfare state—wasn't going to go over well. Even if he wasn't advocating for it. Just suggesting that maybe it wasn't such a bad idea.

Tammy leaned against a table back at the wall. Shure came over and leaned against the table next to her.

"Nice to see you again, Dr. Finklestein," he said.

"Is this normal?" she asked.

"You mean, me alone over here, talking to the new person?" he said. "No. But, then, neither is the talk I gave." He took off his glasses, wiped them with a microfiber. "But I knew that when I wrote it. You'd get this—it was an experiment. I wanted to see for sure what would happen."

"Why do you do it?" she asked Shure. "You don't believe this stuff—they do. Why do you stay? Why not go someplace else?"

"Because I'm needed here," he said. "I wouldn't be needed someplace else. It's my job—part of my job—to try to bring some greater consciousness—awareness of the non-parochial—to the congregation here. Isn't that part of what you do, to?"

"I don't think so," she said.

"With the non-science-majors? With the humanities people you're trying to teach some science to?"

She thought about that. Shure was certainly doing his job with her—getting her to think. She'd never taken that part of her job that seriously. And being stuck with the basketball team—she'd considered that the greatest indignity.

But maybe it wasn't.

I t shouldn't be so hard to find something to publish," Allen said. "If nothing else, you can run some numbers at the computer center, generate a data set, throw something together. Get it online somewhere. Even just get a friend to say something nice about it on the arXiv."

That was part of Allen's MO, Tammy thought. Having paged through the University's research credits in the Web of Knowledge. Lots of data. Some of it repetitive, some of it a little new. Like in materials science—lots of people throwing stuff together, making some kind of new substance, putting it under various electron microscopes; writing it up. Cook and look, they called it.

Tammy had no interest. True science is integrative and imaginative, she thought. Synthetic, in the sense of making something new. Making sense of data and equations; getting at how the universe really works. Having something new to say.

But Allen—and his favorites—had long, long lists of publications in middling journals with nothing much but borderline-novel data. And low Eigen factors.

But. What to actually say to him? "I understand your suggestion," she said. "But I don't think that what I have would get accepted anyplace good."

"It doesn't have to, at this point, Dr. Finkelstein," he said. "Look. Let me tell you a story about how the world works. I don't mean the cynical version where you kiss ass and jump through an arbitrary hoop. I mean networking. Connection building. You submit a paper someplace, an editor sees it, a reviewer reviews it. They send it back to you for revisions or corrections. You make a connection. Now two people who didn't know you before know your name. And you know one of theirs. And, more likely than not, that one reviewer does more than his—more than her fair share of reviewing for that editor. And the next time, you submit to a different journal. And you get known there, and make another contact—someone who knows your work, and not just your name, not just some profile on LinkedIn or elsewhere. And you do it often enough, and fast enough, you've got a list of contacts. And a list of contacts of people who are themselves well connected. Look; I haven't got any illusions that I'm going to be up for a trip to Sweden any time soon. But I got where I am because I know people; and they know me. And that can hep you more—especially if as you claim you've got a long-term project—then someone your age probably realizes."

Later that evening, Tammy decided to take another look at the stuff that Seth had sent. Along with the data sets, Seth had sent a video—when they'd run the experiments, they'd taken some video footage. Of the whole set up; of the subjects; of the camera outputs.

The experiment they'd set up—from a question from a late-night coffee klatsch—was to see if patients with visual cortex implants would consciously perceive a double-slit interference pattern.

These were patients—totally blind, mainly from optic never damage—given a prosthetic implant that sent data from a digital camera to an implant that would stimulate the visual cortex. This was a phase II clinical trial to see if this technology could restore sight, and the initial results were promising.

So what Seth and Tammy—and the PI from the joint MIT/Brigham and Women's group—did was set up a double-slit right in front of the camera lens, so that the light information would feed directly to the implant; and then also ran a feed from the camera to an external monitor.

The material Seth sent: The methods outline, the data table of the patients and their subjective testimony, and the video files, which showed the experiments being done, what the patients said, with the interference pattern on picture-in-picture.

None of the patients perceived the interference pattern. Even as it *clearly* appeared on the external monitor. This implied, to Tammy, a quantum function for consciousness.

That, though, would be quite the leap.

And what Seth *hadn't* sent: Discussion. Conclusion. Abstract. Title.

She sighed. Might as well add the missing parts and see what happens (likely nothing).

So: Discussion. Expected patients to see—scratch that—*perceive*—the interference pattern but the did not.

Conclusion: Unexpected result with non-traditional implications that would need to be replicated.

Introduction: Explain what and why we tried this.

Abstract: We find that people did not consciously perceive an interference pattern in a double-slit experiment fed directly to the visual cortex.

Title: Double-slit photonics information not perceived by visual cortex implants.

References: Really just referencing the visual cortex implant work—there were a few papers published on it.

The manuscript came to about 10 pages in L^{A}T$_{E}$X. She distilled it to PDF and sent it back to Seth.

Three days later, Seth wrote back:
"This looked great. I posted it as a preprint. Oh. And submitted it to NatComms."

NatComms? Tammy thought, with a start. NatComms was short for *Nature Communications,* which was an open access journal. Meaning you had to pay an article-processing charge (APC) to publish. And Tammy had no such funds.

Not to mention—even as a "mega journal," NatComms was hard to get in to.

She wrote back. "Well, I have no APC money. But that won't really matter because it'll get rejected, anyway."

"Don't be so sure," he wrote back, with a link to the paper's preprint—which included the videos as supplemental data. In 48 hours, the paper had gotten 100 views and downloads; and there were 10 comments on it already. Mostly people fascinated that the interference pattern was working properly, but that the patients did not perceive it.

A video call request popped in to the corner of her screen—Allen. She accepted the call and opened the cover on her webcam.

Allen was in his office; the background was blurred but she could make out the outline of his books behind him. He said, "Dr. Finklestein. I've just come across the preprint you wrote with Dr. Howe. Have you submitted it yet?"

"Dean Allen. Dr. Howe just told me he has submitted it to NatComms. But I don't—"

"If you're worried about the APC—don't," he said. "I mean—it'd surprise me if Dr. Howe couldn't come up with his share. But I have some discretionary funds we could use on our side. Interesting work, Dr. Finklestein. When this gets formally published, I think I can arrange a lab upgrade for you. And to continue this—we can link up with Cornell where they're doing similar visual work."

All that from just one article? She thought.

But if Allen was right... She said, "You would be interested in my pursuing this sort of work? Dealing with consciousness?"

"If you can design experiments that get intriguing, valid results and can get published in highly-read places? If it's not illegal you can work on whatever you want. Except that I will probably ask you to file some grant applications."

"Although what we did wasn't expensive."

"I know that. The NSF doesn't—and does not need to."

Tammy took a deep breath. "Could that include going to the APS March meeting?"

"It definitely could—if you don't mind that I am going too." Then Allen paused. "But I know what you're thinking, Dr. Finklestein—this could also be your ticket to a lot of other places."

Right, Tammy thought. He thinks I want to go to the meeting to job hunt. Which would, she thought, likely be a different experience this time around, if what Allen was saying was correct.

He said, "But I do hope you will consider staying here."

One paper—one article—one decision and a probability wave collapsed in one way rather than the other. Opening up other choices. Other could-be's and might-be's. Other lives split off from a single choice. To stay in Binghamton—but not to be staying put. Or to go; and start over yet again.

"I can't say for certain just right now, Dean," she said. "But for now I think I'm inclined to stay out here." She could work in a degree of quiet, with some—but fewer—politics (except at church), away from the bright lights' glare.

Triangulation

When Randy got back from getting his Nobel Prize, what was the first thing he wanted to show me? The medallion? The check? Him in a tux trying to give a speech? No. "Patty— you've got to see this—they *interviewed* me. *Me.* They cut it down to only a few minutes for broadcast, but she put the whole thing up on YouTube."

"OK—wait a minute," I said. "First things first. 'She' who?"

"Heather Kelley—the reporter who interviewed me. We talked for about an hour on camera, then we went out after. It was amazing how much she knew about my work—"

"Randy, look. It's called 'research.' If they're going to send someone all the way to Sweden to interview you—"

"Look, do you want to see the video or not?"

We were out at my house in Waltham—I've got a wall-sized LED on the far wall (I watch with sound off when I'm mixing audio—distracts my eyes so my ears can work). So we pulled up the Tube video, shunted it to the big screen, and ran the audio through my studio monitors.

And there it was. Heather Kelley—as if you couldn't tell from the name—in life-size HD—very Irish. She was a good interviewer, too. I could tell, the way she was pulling Randy out of himself for the interview. I mean, I'd been interviewed enough in my day. But I could see Randy, sitting in my studio, watching the video. And I don't think he thought that's all it was.

They sat in one of those faux living rooms, facing each other in comfortable chairs. The video wasn't entirely raw—the sound had been worked on (I could obviously tell) and they'd put "the crawl" across the bottom, feeding news from the 12 of December, 2023.

"So can you explain to everyone out there about the work that you did that the Nobel Committee chose to honor?"

"We'd had this idea," Randy, on the video, said. "You know about the uncertainty principle, right? So I wanted to see if I could track a particle by both entangling it and then tracking the original particle and the entangled particle separately. When we got contradictory results, I thought the particles got disentangled. And then Sally—my grad student—looked at the results and said, no, dummy, it's what you'd get if you pulled in a particle from somewhere else. Then we did the math, wrote it up, and a few others reproduced the experiment. And—except for some complicated wave math, that's it."

"And how do you do that?" she asked.

"You triangulate the particles—three lasers, magnetic bottle—kind of technical."

"So how soon before we're stepping into alternate realities?" Her eyes twinkled—I'm convinced she could do it on command.

Randy paused, looked at his hands. "That's just science fiction—really—we're just dealing with photons and electrons. Not people."

She gave a condescending smile—like she should condescend to a Nobel laureate. And she said, "Well, if you *did* go to another universe, would anybody know?"

Randy, to his credit, gave a condescending smile right back. Probably, I thought, he was used to getting those kinds of questions when he did parents' weekend or intro classes. He said, "The you in the other universe wouldn't have any idea. Only the person who actually moved between realities would know."

And that was that. For a little while, anyway. Later, I thought, I should have seen it—I could have put some of the pieces together. But I actually had a *life* to attend to. Or a career. Or a wound-down career, at any rate. At least, that was the perspective of my agent.

A long time ago—Was it that long ago? 10 years, I guess. 10 years ago, I was 25. And I'd written a number-one album. The album took 10 years to write—they were the best years of my life, Billy Joel would say—I started on the family upright when I was fifteen. Hooked up with some people at college—one had an expensive interface and DAW, another had a killer voice. We made a few demos and sent them around, played a few gigs, and, I thought, that would be that.

But when I graduated, I had a contract. I got co-producer credit, though I did almost all the work—including about 90% of the instruments and about 70% of the engineering. The album went platinum. And I found that I couldn't write music—well, not *good* music—on command or on schedule. And I found it easy to live comfortably off of the interest on my royalties (I invested heavily in munis). But the kicker was that the guys at the label knew who'd really produced the record. And even though I suffered writer's block, I get constant production work.

So that's what I do. Conservatory-trained ears, and I try to add a little depth to the recordings of four-chord wonders.

Anyway, for the next few weeks I only heard from Randy by Internet. I was locked down, producing some sessions for a supposedly up-and-coming local band for nearly a month. So when I finally got a break, I decided to swing by Randy's lab at MIT.

I found him sitting at his computer in the lab, so distracted he didn't hear me come in. I snuck up behind him, to read his screen over his shoulder. And the first thing I saw was the 9x12 glossy of Heather Kelley propped up on his desk. Autographed, no less—"With luv, Heather." Gotta love that—a journalist who can't spell.

"So, what's this?" I asked.

He jumped. "God, Patty—don't *do* that!"

"Well, if you were paying more attention to the world around you… So, what exactly is it that's so snared your attention?"

"My next project," he said. "See if we can swap more than one particle at a time. Maybe even a macro-sized object."

"And in English, that means…?"

"Bringing in a clump of dust from a different universe to this one. Which also as a consequence means sending a clump of dust from this universe to the other one."

And at about this time, not only was I trying to rescue the debut recordings of three new discoveries, but I'd found that I was actually becoming able to piece together my own songs. It'd been about ten years—that was about right, I figured. So my attention was fixed elsewhere most of the time. Otherwise I might have noticed how often and with how much fascination Randy talked about Heather. Or about how much time they seemed to spend together. Especially considering that Heather was engaged.

And *that*, I'm sure, I didn't know until too late. And I'm sure I wouldn't have known, even if I'd been paying attention, because Randy wasn't about to tell me until it turned out that he absolutely *had* to. Because Heather's fiancé *had* been paying attention. And said fiancé—a retired halfback for the Patriots—had noticed his fiancée hanging around with this nerdy scientist, and had gotten suspicious. So Randy, to save his skin, told them he had a girlfriend—namely, me. And wouldn't they love to meet me.

And when Randy explained all this to me—by way of asking if I'd do this one *really big* favor for him—I thought to ask, "So, what is it with this Heather woman, anyway?" And that's when things got strange.

"Patty—I don't know. I've never felt like this before—about anyone."

We were walking from Randy's office—on the promenade along the Charles in front of MIT—on our way to meet Heather and Jack for dinner. They were sending a limo for us—we were supposed to meet the car just off campus.

"You know," I said, "generally speaking, it's good form—if you're going to fall in love—to fall for someone who isn't already involved."

"I know. But I don't know if I had a choice. And if she's so in love with him, how come there's anything between *us*?"

I stopped short, and turned on him. "What do you mean? For one thing, there *isn't* anything between you—"

"There *is*. When we're together."

"You think that because you think you feel something, that it's *because* she feels it too?"

He looked at me as if I'd just said something incredibly, stupidly obvious—like, "you mean the Earth is an oblong spheroid?"

"Shouldn't that be obvious?" he asked. "I mean, if not, then where is it coming from? Doesn't this 'chemistry' have to be mutual?"

Oh, Randy… "Randy—if that were true—there'd be no such thing as a broken heart." And I started walking again.

He fell a little behind, apparently, I guess, giving that some thought. Anyway, I got to the car first. He caught up, the driver let us in, and we were off.

The car was nice, and new. Not the fanciest limousine I'd ever been in, but still. It had the new car smell—and you could still smell the new leather from the upholstery. The last time I was chauffeured around like this was to and from concerts. The smell—the leather—brought that back. And in a way, I thought, although not a concert, this evening was a type of performance, too.

I looked over at Randy. He was fiddling with his hands—the way he does when he's nervous. Though I can't believe I *know* that.

I've known Randy virtually all of my adult life. We were hall-mates, Freshman year at Tufts. Though, we didn't get to know each other until almost the end of finals, first semester. I was in the joint program with the New England Conservatory, and Randy… Well, I guess he spent most of his time in the library, or the lab, or somewhere studying. Not only is he naturally brilliant, but he works—*hard*. Harder than I *ever* worked at anything.

Anyway, the first time either of us had any significant time to hang around our rooms was after our tests were finished. And most of the floor had already left for winter break. So one night I went to the lounge to watch TV, and Randy was already there. And we started talking—and kept talking literally all night. And we've been… whatever it is we are… ever since.

The car pulled up at a trendy hot spot near the Hines Center. Heather and Jack were already there, waiting for us. They looked good—they both looked good. *And* they looked good together. Heather wore green—which I'd notice later went with her eyes. Jack was tall. With a tousle of sandy hair. With nice eyes. And a nice chin—good cheekbones.

We went in, and got settled. Randy on my left, Heather on my right. And after they took our order, Heather turned to me, and said, "So you've been together since college?"

"Uh…" I said. "We've *known* each other since college. This… this is rather… recent…"

"Oh, I see," Heather said. "With Jack and me, it was love at first sight. Wasn't it?" she asked him.

"And how did *that* happen?" I asked.

"Well. I drew what I thought would be a boring assignment—a human interest interview of some jocks—"

"Hey!" interjected Jack.

"Sorry, sweetie. You know I didn't mean it that way. Anyway, these *athletes* were volunteering community service—working with troubled youth, etcetera. And Jack was one of them. And the rest, as they say, was history."

"And how long is that history?" I asked.

"Huh?" Jack asked.

I resisted the impulse to repeat the question slow and loud. Kind of like shooting fish in a barrel, I thought. "What I meant was," I said, "was how long have you been together?"

"Oh. A little more than three years," Jack said.

Our first course was served—I'd gotten a French onion soup—big round crock, bread melted over with cheese. Randy ate bread. Jack got oysters, or clams, or something in a shell. Heather, of course, ordered a salad. And halfway through the salad, she excused herself.

When she'd gone, Jack turned to me. "So, you're really *the* Patty Glaser? From Dream Ark? I was a big fan."

"Thanks," I said, a little sheepishly.

"I must have played that album a million times. My favorite on the album was one of the ballads—'Unrequited.' Did you write that?"

"Yes," I said. "Yes, I did."

He got a wistful look in his eye. "I lost my virginity to that song."

Great. Wonderful. Thanks. Over dinner. That was an image I just *really* didn't need.

"Excuse me," I said, "I think I need to visit the ladies' room as well."

I washed my hands, and splashed water on my face. Drying my cheeks, I stared into the mirror. What a bizarre evening. I stared into my own pupils. What a weird combination, this, I thought. Blonde hair, brown eyes. Short end of the stick on both counts, in my opinion. If my parents *had* to split the genes, couldn't I have gotten it the other way—dark hair and blue eyes—like the Deschanel sisters or Courtney Cox?

I heard the stall behind me open, and out came Heather.

"Hey," she said. "Did you leave them out there by themselves?"

"No," I said. "I asked the busboy to babysit."

She giggled. "I love your wit. You know, come to think of it, I'd love to do a feature on *you*. Do you have anything new in the works? You're too good for a 'where are they now' piece."

I leaned with my back against the sink, looking her over. Maybe I'd misjudged her. "Yeah, maybe," I said. I didn't want to do the whole cliché thing—been working on some things, have things in the fire/oven/what-have-you.

"'Maybe?'" she asked. "Well, do you or don't you?"

"I've been writing songs," I said. "But I don't know if I'll be able to place it. Who remembers a one-album act from ten years ago? And my lead singer's a lawyer now—I *think*. And I think she has kids—"

"It was the songs, not the singer," she said. "And with the Internet—you could put out your demos, low cost, and see what happens. And, plus, a TV feature would be a good place to start."

"And what's *your* angle?" I asked.

"Haven't got one," she said. "Except for filling my segments with items more interesting than what my producer finds."

"That's it? No hidden story—no trying to find drug abuse and addiction in my past—which you won't by the way."

"Not at all," she said. "I know lots of my colleagues would be. But I do the 'fluff pieces' they won't do, because I *don't* want to go there." This time, she stared at me, looking me up and down. "You're so unlike Randy. How did you get together, anyway?"

That was a good question. Considering that Randy hadn't actually made anything up or coached me. "It just kind of… happened," I said.

"You're very lucky, you know," she said. "I've never spent so much time with someone so interesting."

Yeah, interesting. That's an understatement. "And that's why you seem to be spending so much time with him?"

"Well, yes," she said. "Why else?"

"There wouldn't be any… *other* reasons?" I asked, trying to sound suspicious.

The shadow of a scowl briefly crossed her sunny features before it fled. "You're not jealous, are you?"

"And if I was?" I asked.

"Well, there's nothing like that going on. And even if there was—you're Patty Glaser. You hung on a million boys' dorm-room walls. Who could compete with that?"

Yeah, who indeed, I thought.

I walked an unusually quiet Randy back to MIT after dinner.

"I don't understand," he said. "I don't see it."

"Don't see what?" I asked.

"Why she's with the steroid case," he said. "I don't get it. I could think circles—no—*spheres*—around that guy."

"And, what? You want to know why she's with him, and not with you?" I asked.

He nodded.

"Randy, you could think spheres around *anybody*. It goes with the whole Nobel thing. But it's—"

"Well," he said, "Not *everyone*. Not you."

And, to my embarrassment, I actually felt myself flush at that. But I continued. "But it's not necessarily about that. It's—"

"So what is it about?" he asked.

I hit on an idea. "Is Heather as accomplished as you?" I asked.

"No, but…"

"But what?"

He paused. "OK—OK, you've made your point." He put his hands in his pockets, and stared out at the river. "Still, I think there's something there. And I *know* that if it weren't for Jack… If she hadn't met Jack first, things would have worked out."

There is a fine line between love and illusion—a line from an old Rush song—crossed my mind—*the lens between wishes and fact.* "You don't know that," I said. "You *can't* know that. For all you know, Heather and Jack were meant to be together, and the timing of it was just details."

"I do not believe that," he said. "There are nine billion people on this planet, and each of our paths intersects with hundreds—thousands—of others every day. Anything can happen—hinged on probability, like any other phenomenon. I cannot buy into the idea that two people are somehow destined for each other, irrespective of chance and effort."

"Chance is exactly the point!" he said. "A probability wave collapsed in one state instead of the other and the cat lives. If you could re-do exactly the circumstances, but another time having the state that could go either way go the *this* way instead of *that* way."

I rubbed my eyes. It sounded to me like he was saying he could turn Justin Bieber into Rush—just because they're all Canadian, and regardless of anything else. I didn't know what else to say to Randy—about how Heather fit with Jack. How he and I ought to fit. I thought, I should resent Heather, that she was filling his field of vision. But I knew better than that—for ten years, if it hadn't been one thing, it had been another. I could see the appeal of what he was saying. But it was just another way of saying, "if only…" And I said, "Look. Here's the bottom line, and I'll say it as someone who's written it. 'If only' works only in song."

"As a poetic conceit—that's probably true," he said. "And for most people—who lack the capacity to change their circumstances—change their luck—that's definitely true." He looked out at the river, and said, "I've just had a thought—something I want to get down before I forget it—I'm going to peel off here; stop in at the lab."

At this point, I was just as happy to drop him at his lab, and catch a taxi home.

Randy handled today better than I would have, I think. Especially considering that he'd turned down Heather and Jack's request that he be their best man. I'm not sure what she was thinking, in the first place, asking an old boyfriend to be the best man at her wedding. Especially when, at that wedding, she was marrying the guy she'd dumped Randy for in the first place.

I stood out on the ballroom terrace looking out over Christian Science plaza in the early December chill, staring at the calendar entry on my phone—the "meeting invite" Randy had sent me when he'd asked me—"Heather and Jack, December 3, 2011."

Most people might have found that an odd way to ask someone to be their date for a wedding. But I've been either on the road or in a studio somewhere for most of the last ten years. So the Internet's been a lifesaver. And career-saver, I thought. The Net lets me put out songs and vids, one at a time, without having to worry about "finishing" and "album." I'd probably have been creatively *paralyzed* without it. I'd probably have turned into one of those washed-up musician-turned-producer people.

Randy found me on the terrace. "They're almost ready to start with the cake," he said.

"You OK?" I asked.

"Yeah, why?"

"You look a little lost," I said.

"I was thinking about Sweden," he said. "I've only ever spoken before in front of students or other physicists—the biggest audience was at the American Physical Society March Meeting three years ago. I'm a little nervous about making this speech next week."

"I'm sure you'll be fine," I said. "And I'm sure that's not the only reason you're out here."

"OK—how about, crowds of strangers make me uncomfortable?"

"Those aren't strangers—they're the celebrities of Boston—I think I might've even seen a Kennedy or two..."

He smiled. "By the way, I really liked the song you wrote for them. Your voice sounded good."

"Heather insisted that I sing it. She thinks it'll be good exposure for me. And for her, to be honest."

"Yeah." And then, silence. "They seem happy, together," he said.

"Well, that's a very healthy observation for you to be making," I replied.

"I'd thought about it a lot. You once said that if two people were supposed to be together, they would be."

"I never said that..."

"I'm sure you did..." he said. "I know I heard it somewhere... Anyway, I've been thinking about that—pretty much ever since they got engaged. And I was thinking about the ways people's paths interconnect and intersect, and about the chances of people finding each other in a planet of nine billion. And I was thinking that sometimes that what you find is in the last place you look, and the last place you look is right in front of you."

Well, I thought, I could probably get a song or two out of *that*. What I said, was, "What are you saying?"

"I'm saying—I'm wondering—if maybe you think we should go somewhere quiet to talk for a while after this?"

I thought about that for a second. And then I said, "Yeah. Maybe we should."

The Tower in the Tunnel

So, there I was, with a needle in my arm. No, not in the execution room of the penitentiary. At a portable setup rigged in my "business partner's" laboratory. So that he could do his research thing by taking advantage of knowing exactly when and how I would die.

Was I guilty? Hell, yes. Of murder? Hell, no. But my problem was that I had a history of aliases and shady dealings. Which was why Norman Pitcher—*Professor* Norman Pitcher, watching this happen in his own lab—had first recruited me. Ten years ago, I was on parole, in a half-way house when Norman went looking for me. Looking for me? He was a distant cousin; not by blood but by marriage. And he knew enough about my past and my aliases that he thought I might suit his needs. He'd first found me at the coffee house where I was working.

He'd walked in, not looking any different from any of the other SoHo coffee addicts. Mid-50s looking with wispy straw hair flying around a bare crown; faded jeans; dress shirt; black suit jacket; rimless glasses. So similar to all the other middle-aged men still addicted to over-priced coffee that I hadn't noticed him, even when he was at the counter, until he called me by name.

"Alex Grey?" he asked.

My *real* name. I was going by Zack Blanco by that time. So that got my attention. Real fast. "Do you have a badge?" I asked.

He smiled sheepishly. "No. We have a familial connection. When is your shift complete? That is, when could we speak briefly?"

"I'm on 4-to-8," I said, "And then straight back to the halfway house."

"Would you be permitted to make a detour in the case that the conversation could center on an improved employment situation?"

At that point, I wasn't sure if he was going to actually offer me a job, or only *discuss* one as a work-around. But, maybe… "Could be," I said. "Would this discussion involve dinner?"

"It can, yes," he said.

"Fine, then," I said. "Meet me back here at 8; we're open 24/7, so you wouldn't be waiting around outside."

"Very good," he said. "And, also, I'd like to try one of those lattes; a very large one." Then he left with his coffee.

Later, over dinner, he explained what he was up to; and where I might fit in. Kind of creeped me out, the first time I heard it. But when I thought about it a little, I couldn't say I wasn't interested in helping. Not just for the money; and not just for the challenge; but I wanted to know, too. I think everyone alive, everyone who knows that someday they'll die, I think everyone would want to know.

Anyway. He was waiting for me on the corner outside the coffee bar. Sixth and Varick—neighborhood full of big ware-housy-like buildings lining the approach to the Holland Tunnel. Very industrial. When I was getting released to the halfway house, I did some reading up on where I'd be. What I read said that there used to be a lot printing companies in those blocky buildings, back when you had to print a whole lot of copies for printing anything to make sense. Now a lot of those buildings were being used for storage, since, even when you want something on paper, they can run it off for you one at a time.

We walked up to a place on Downing and Bedford.

"Will this do?" Pitcher asked. "You should be able to get back to Chelsea on the 1 Train or the C or E around the corner."

I nodded. The halfway house was in a townhouse in Chelsea where the landlord defaulted on his taxes and was seized by the City. None of the neighbors realized what it was. They would see only men coming and going, and I guess they assumed we were all gay, given the neighborhood.

People make assumptions about me all the time. I stopped caring about that in jail.

We walked in, sat down. Then, "How often do you think about what happens when you die?" Pitcher asked, over soup.

"Mostly, I spend most of my time thinking about how to survive," I said. I thought about it once in a while. Not my problem just now; and when it became my problem, there really wasn't much I could do about it.

"Fair enough," Pitcher said. He looked down at his hands, and went quiet for a while.

Great relief to me—I just dug into my burger and fries. Talk about a burger! This wasn't a fast-food joint, but an upscale place. They made hamburger out of prime quality sirloin. And homemade shoestring fries. Not the kind of place I would've spent my own money on.

"Perhaps I should approach this from a different angle," he said. "Maybe I should tell you something about myself, and from there lead into what I am hoping you can do for me."

"OK," I shrugged. I felt ketchup drip down my chin and I reached for the napkin.

"I am a high energy physicist, specifically particles and strings; I have a position at CUNY on 34th Street, when I am here in New York. I spend a significant portion of my time at the LHC, and some other time in Chicago. My published research, at this point, has focused on the detection of negative matter."

"Negative matter?" I asked. "You mean anti-matter?"

"Anti-matter is different," he said. "Anti-matter is particles with opposite charges. Negative matter interacts with space-time in the opposite way from regular matter."

"Right. Of course," I said, not understanding in the least.

"Not important right now," he said. "But another interest of mine is near-death experiences."

"The tunnel, the light, the relatives' voices?"

"Yes. That's it exactly," he said. "What would you say if I said I had a hypothesis of what could be happening there?"

"I would say that I bet they've got a whole file—that they've completely figured that out—and you could probably find out about it in New Mexico," I said.

"I doubt that," he replied. "They only handle extraterrestrials."

His expression, tone of voice, matched mine a few minutes ago when I made like I understood about the anti-negative whatever it was.

I was starting to like this guy.

He went on. "The key thing is, I have an experiment that I could conduct on death or near-death."

I thought about that. If he was talking about trying to run some kind of experiment on someone when they were dying, he'd have to know exactly when and where someone was dying. And, really, the only way to *really* know that is to kill them yourself. I said, "How are you going to do that without putting yourself in line for a needle yourself?"

He smiled, and nodded. "That's exactly what I need you for."

I still wasn't sold on the whole idea by then; so he had me come up to this place in Morningside Heights—some big warehouse-sized lab at 135th, west of Broadway. Some big research complex they'd built in the 2010s—I'd read about the big fight that had gone on before they built it. There'd been a bunch of business out there that had put a good fight against the universities, but had ended up losing; and they built this whole new big research complex.

A girl in faded blue jeans and a blue sweater met me outside the building.

"You're Zack?" she asked. I couldn't help noticing that her eyes matched her jeans.

"That's me," I said. "Who're you?"

"Joanne Marshall; I'm a post-doc with Professor Pitcher's group." She looked me up and down, trying not to look like she was checking me out. I'm six feet, and I wear a 42 jacket and 30 waist; women do that a lot. The way I saw it, I wouldn't have a chance with her anyway. I figured she assumed I was an idiot, because I only went to a State College and never graduated. Never mind about the 10 years I spent killing time working my way through the NYPL's online collection.

She led me past the front desk, and down two flights of stairs to a mid-level basement. The lab looked to take up at least the entire building block. At least? I couldn't tell, it looked like there could have been parts extending further underground. But I couldn't tell from the office area where Joanne led me.

We were waiting in an open area, maybe 20 by 20, surrounded by lab benches, some kinds of shiny equipment I couldn't recognize, and lots and lots of computer screens, and computer pads laying around on the tables. Off to the right were a row of offices with white doors and glass walls. In the third office, through the glass, I could see Pitcher talking to a tall, reedy man in a lab coat. He saw us through the window, and wrapped up his conversation. He opened the door and let the other guy out. Then, "Zack. Good to see you. Come in."

"You're up," Joanne said to me. "Good luck."

Good luck? I thought, *with* this *guy?* He didn't come out to where I was, just stood in the office threshold, waiting for me to come to him.

I walked into the office. Maple-colored door and glass wall facing the lab area. Big blank white cinderblock wall on the other side. We were underground, so, no window. Ergonomic white L-shaped desk; the side facing the wall to the right was plastered with computer monitors; the wall to the left had one really big monitor. On the desk, a traditional keyboard on the right side. A few animated picture frames, and also a computer pad on the main part of the desk. Two comfortable chairs in front; a weave-task chair behind. Pitcher himself was in jeans with worn shoes and a dress shirt about a size or two too tight, covered with a lab coat. "Nice digs," I said.

"They are," he said, "but not because of the furnishings." He paused. "And, thanks. And I am gratified you could make it. I think this will be a very interesting partnership."

"I haven't quite agreed to that yet, doc," I said. Wasn't sure why I started calling him "Doc." Must have been the lab coat. "I came down here to find out first what it is you want. Then I'll decide if I'm in."

He smiled broadly, and motioned toward one of the guest chairs. "Oh, I am certain after you see what this is about you'll want to be a part of it," he said. "Please have a seat; I have something I want to show you." He sat down in the desk chair, and picked up the tablet. The lights went down, and the big monitor to powered up. "I want you to see this—this is still rough; it is something I have been collaborating with Cosmos.com on."

"That who the other guy was?" I asked.

"As a matter of fact, yes," Pitcher said. "We were going over the next step in this—we're working on a three-part series they're going to stream. This bit is only about five minutes long and it's written for a general audience, so I hope it can explain a bit more about what we're working on here than I can." He touched the pad and started the clip.

What it talked about, with a lot of snazzy computer graphics, was how what they used to call dark matter and dark energy really are another universe butting up against ours. That the two universes are so close that pieces of them interfere with each other.

Pitcher touched the tablet again and the lights came up. "So?"

"Interesting," I said. "Should be popular. Not sure what it has to do with me, though."

"Right," he said. "Now, the other areas I work in. I have also been working on a quantum string/complexity theory of consciousness."

"Oh, yes. Of course," I said.

"Right. Suffice it to say that all it is is looking at pieces of the fundamental structure and motion of the universe that, if we're right, give rise to self-directing and subjective consciousness."

"What's that have to do with the alternate universe stuff?"

"Well, I assume you've heard about near-death experiences?"

"Yeah, sure I have," I said. It's a cliché, the tunnel and the light and all that.

"What if, when you die, your consciousness goes to that other universe?" he asked. "That's the question I am working on—at least, in my free time."

"Yeah, but, that would have to be just speculation, right? There'd be no way to really find out."

"There *could* be a way," he said. "Theoretically, it should be possible to create a wormhole through. However, trying to make a wormhole from *this* universe to that one would take more energy than humans are likely to have for millions of years. My thinking is this: If this is true—if the information from our experiences is imported into this neighboring universe, then it must be *pulled* from that side, rather than *pushed* from this one; and the attendant wormhole must be like a valve—easy to open from that reality, very, very hard to open from *this* one. So what I want to do is, when the passage might be open, send a small probe through."

"You mean, like the Aphrodite probe that they just sent to Venus?" I'd seen that on the news. Thing was nothing more really than a balloon, floating in the clouds over Venus. They said they might be sending astronauts to meet up with it at some point.

"Similar in intent," Pitcher said. "Much different in construction." He touched the pad again. On the monitor, there was a model. It was a bunch of colored balls, stuck together, spinning. "A collection of entangled particles— entangled with particles at the other end of a fiber optic pipe, that is. From which we can collect data. This model here is just a collection of stabilized quarks—this isn't even the size of a proton."

So I was walking this through my head. You send this thing through this wormhole, and you find out—I guess you find out what Hell is like? I suppose if I was more of an optimist, I'd say Heaven. Well, really, I'm a realist—split the difference at Purgatory or Limbo.

But if this tunnel only opens from the *other* side... "So, wait. If you were going to do this, you'd have to know when this valve was going to open, right? So, really, you'd have to be there when someone was dying or having a near-death experience."

Pitcher slapped his desk and nearly jumped out of his chair. "That's it! That's it *exactly*! You've got it. And now you see the trickiest part of this experiment. How do you predict one of the unpredictable things?"

"What about executions?" I asked. They didn't apply the death penalty to much; but even getting toward the 22nd Century, we had it.

"I investigated that," he said. "I could not get any Department of Justice—not in the 15 states with a death penalty or the Federal—to allow this experiment."

"So what is that you wanted me to do?" I asked. I was really hoping by this point that he didn't want *me* to kill anyone, either. I ran a Synthiate lab and an Internet numbers ring from my dorm room in college. I was decent at the chemistry and very good at the math. *That* was enough to get me 10 years in state prison, with another 10 of probation still hanging over me.

"I would like you to infiltrate the hospice at the New York Teaching Hospital. And I'll pay you a research stipend of 100,000 Unios per year until we can conduct a complete experiment."

I narrowed my eyes. Good money. But... "That's a generous number. But that's not going to work. Even in a hospice you can't tell the exact time someone's going to die."

"Unless they're opting for assisted suicide," he said.

Assisted suicide had become legal in 2032. Had to be performed under strict controls—there were legal requirements and checks. Sounded like a good idea in theory. Except that it was missing a key real-world fact. Pitcher seemed so caught up in his particles and his big questions that he was missing how things really play out.

"Not going to work," I said. "People go for AS when they're in *pain*. When they're in a hospice—if they're doing it right—they *shouldn't* be in pain. And I'd assume that the outfit at New York Teaching is pretty good." As it is one of the best hospitals in the world.

Pitcher sat back down, slumped in his chair. He looked away, disappointed. He apparently hadn't thought this through in terms of how people act.

I turned the other way, and looked out the window-wall to the common lab area. Joanne was holding court—smart, pretty girl surrounded mostly by men. I thought about what her life would be like if she suddenly found herself in a female-dominated domain; having to compete for men's attentions instead. Would be a big change. And from this, I was thinking about what would inspire someone to want to get an AS. Frustration with loss of abilities? Pain? What? Maybe being in aggressive treatment that wasn't working? Maybe in experimental treatments? No, on that. They'd probably be screened out. But: Someone almost certainly terminal, but not certain enough that people around him—or her—would be pushing aggressive treatments.

And with most cancers and heart disease under control, what did that leave? Alzheimer's? Maybe that would be the place to start—neuro research. I turned back to Pitcher, and said: "So. What if someone was forced into treatments they didn't want? Maybe something experimental on something still terminal? Maybe someone like that would opt for an AS while they still had their minds."

Pitcher looked at me; the idea catching fire across his puffy face. "Yes. That could be it. An experimental neuroscience ward?"

"Yeah. Something like that," I said.

"So, not the hospice at New York Teaching. But the Neurology wing... I'll do a literature search; make sure it's the best place. And I still have a contact in the HR department at the hospital."

And that was how I wound up working as an orderly at the Meryl Pavilion for Neurological Disorders at the New York Teaching Hospital in lower Washington Heights.

The second week after I got the gig at the hospital, I walked into the lab, looking for Pitcher for our weekly meeting. Joanne met me in the common area.

"Professor Pitcher asked me to look after you," she said.

"Look after me?"

"It's budget season," she said. "Pitcher gets funding for the University. He's been doing this the last fifteen years. He's developed such a good network in DC that if he wanted to give up on physics, he could open a firm on K Street."

Never thought that geeks would have to be political, that way. None of those science books I read as a kid ever mentioned that. And I was going to say so, when she turned on her Tab.

"So. I wanted to get a sense of where we stand so far," she said. "I know you're not a violent offender, so do we need to find someone else who would be able to find someone who does AS?"

How'd she know my record? I wanted to know, so I asked.

"I looked you up on LawNet," she said.

I'd used LawNet at the prison library. I wanted to know how I could get paroled quickly. Easy to find stuff. Not so easy to cut through the legalese.

"You know how to do that?"

"I figured it out," she said. "I do have a Ph.D. in quantum information. Anyway, you got what I would consider a bad deal on things that ought to be legal, anyway. So I'm not sure if you know the kinds of people we'd need."

She'd kind of rubbed me the wrong way, the first day I came there. Too lucky, maybe. Too, I don't know, maybe like she was proud that she was too straight. Like everything would come easy to her, when it didn't come easy to the rest of us. But her last comment, about things that should be legal, that I didn't expect.

Now, the thing she was asking about—did I know people who could do Assisted Suicide—the short answer was "yes." The thing about AS. It was like smoking. It was legal, but you wouldn't want people to know you were doing it. So the guys who did it didn't tend to advertise on the Internet. (And those that did; well; you'd want to stay away from.) If your loved one was in that situation, and you wanted someone, you'd want recommendations.

So, yeah. After five years in jail, and still living in the halfway house, I knew people who knew people. In particular, a guy based in Philly with a clean record.

"I've done some research," I said, answering her question. "I can get someone when it's time."

"Wow. OK," she said. "Wasn't expecting that. So; you could let that be known at the hospital, too?"

Which would then automatically get the people looking into AS talking to me. "That's the plan," I said. "Already being taken care of."

Most of the stuff going on the ward was outpatient. There were a few experiments and studies going on where people would get implants and maybe stay for a few days after surgery. But, other than that, mostly it was outpatient.

Except for some of the research into Alzheimer's and prion disease. And those people were pretty bad off.

I don't know how people do it, when they're not getting paid. I mean cleaning up other people's waste. I didn't mind running medicines up from the formulary; or pushing people around on stretchers; or any of the other basically manual labor. It was pretty mindless, but it gave me time to think about other things.

But the cleaning up—changing sheets of people who couldn't hold it anymore. That was the worst part. When you do that for someone and it's not your job, you must really love them. And I don't mean for babies, either. There's a huge difference between changing the diaper of a 7-pound baby and changing the diaper of a 200-pound man.

I could handle the babies.

Dr. Stein—an old guy maybe getting toward 100—was in charge of that part of the department. I hardly ever saw him but I saw a lot of his patients. Mostly, they were rich, and mostly they—and their families—were willing to spend vast sums on hope. In the end, the money they were spending— coming out of those families' inheritances, for what that's worth—was paying for all the research that everyone was hoping would help everyone else. But that insurance or National Health wouldn't pay for.

One of the patients on the wing was a nice old woman, Thea Stella. That is, when she was lucid, she was sweet. And even in the short time I was there those lucid periods were getting shorter. But when she was on, she was *on*. Real sharp. She'd tell me about her kids—about how they thought she didn't know how they were, but that she wanted to change her will to cut must of their inheritance. But she hadn't had the heart to do it.

Anyway, there was Thea. She was on one of the experimental treatments. This one that she was on was some kind of gene therapy—had something to do with getting brain cells to make enzymes to eat the brain plaque.

She'd been a lawyer, before. High-powered corporate defense, I think. Anyway, by the time I got there, she seemed to be doing better more often than before. The other guys on the ward told me she'd been a real basket case when they first brought her in.

"You don't look like you belong here," she said to me, one of her better days. I was changing her bed. This being one of her better days, it was just changing one set of linens for another; no biggie. Plus, she got herself off the bed and into one of the chairs.

She sat there, legs crossed, a tablet balanced on her knee, reading glasses at the end of her nose.

"Neither do you," I said to her.

"Well, not today," she said. "I can see from my chart that I don't always have such good days." She put the tablet on the night table. "But what I mean is that you seem smarter than the average orderly. More like a nurse or PA," she said. "But you don't seem to have the medical training."

"I've got three semesters at a state university, and ten years of New York's cinderblock college," I said.

"Jail? Really? What for?"

"SynthEndorphins. And numbers."

"Jail for that? I think you were ill-served by your representation," she said.

"The lawyer?" I said. "I didn't have any money; I got a public defender. She seemed OK. They DA said I could have been looking at 20 years at a max security. She got me 5 at a minimum." Seemed like a good deal at the time.

"She told you to take the prosecutor's first offer. Probably overworked and underpaid. She must have thought she was doing you a favor by getting you into the minimum security. An average attorney could have gotten you parole. I could have gotten your charges dropped. How did you get caught?"

"The new boyfriend of an ex-girlfriend," I said.

She nodded. "Right. And they said he was going to testify that you'd been violent?"

I nodded.

"Pure crap. Wouldn't have gone to trial. And if it had, if I'd been your counsel, I'd have filleted him on the stand."

I finished with bed, giving the pillow an extra fluff. "There you go, Ms. Stella," I said. "See you tomorrow."

"I hope so," she said.

I knew what she meant.

One Tuesday, about three weeks since Thea was last lucid, I was supervising; watching as the housekeeping machines did their thing with the floors and the unoccupied . They would roll into a room and one would hold the patient while the other one made the bed and took care of the other stuff. Anyway, in burst a man and a woman.

The woman: hair unnaturally black—almost blue-black—over ice blue eyes. The powdered-over wrinkles made her look older than maybe she was. The guy was a little shorter; with dark hair going gray; same ice-blue eyes. They broke into the room like napoleons, scattering nurses and orderlies in their wake. "Are you Zack?" the woman asked.

"Yeah, OK, sure," I said. "Who wants to know?"
"I'm Heather Stella Jones. This is my brother Mike. We've heard you've been helping take care of our mother."

"Sure," I said. "I watch the robots do the hard stuff."

Not even a smile from either of them. They didn't even seem to notice the robots; they were just looking at me, not paying attention to anything else going on in the room. Even as their mother was being taken care of and cleaned by those robots. Looking back, that should have been my clue. Most relatives showed up more than once in six months. And complained about every tiny detail—like, the sheets were the wrong color or the soup was too hot—around their loved ones.

Not these two.

"Can I help you with something?" I asked.

"Perhaps you can," Heather said. "Is there someplace we can talk?"

"Yeah," I said. "Down the hall." I led them to the ward's main waiting room. A hospital waiting room isn't the sort of place you tend to pay much attention to when you're in it. Only later, after the thing you were waiting for has happened do the details seem to matter. This one had been re-done recently. Fresh hardwood floors, newish carbon-fiber chairs with synthfoam stuffing. Big window looking out on the Hudson on one wall, big 3TV on the other with sound off, projecting 24-hour news three feet into the room. We sat catty-corner, me on one side, the two of them on the other.

Heather began. "So you've been here for…"

"Six months," I said.

"You must have seen how our mother has been declining even in that short time," she said.

"She's lucid sometimes," I said.

"Less frequently," she said. She produced a tablet from her bag, pulled up a document, and handed it to me. "She didn't want to linger in a state like this," she said. And the document she showed me said so, too. With Thea's signature at the bottom.

I shrugged.

"We heard from some people that you might be able to get us in contact with someone who could do something about this," the brother, Mike, said.

"I might," I said. This was what I'd been waiting for, assuming this was legit. Get them in touch with this guy, Stu, that I'd found, they make the arrangements. And then the catch… "If you are interested, and if you're sure this is what your mother wants, I can get you in touch with a guy. Licensed and everything."

They looked at each other, seemingly relieved. "That's great news," Heather said. "How soon?"

S omething don't seem right about this," I said. We were sitting in the lab's common area, the three of us, Joanne, Pitcher, and me. Eating Chinese food from a take-out place on 181st Street; one of those places that's just a counter and a two tables, and that's all. But really good food. I'd told them about the Stellas and about how they thought they wanted to do the AS.

"What's not right?" Pitcher said. "This is exactly what we're looking for."

"I don't buy that Thea Stella really signed off on this," I said. "Not when she was lucid."

"Then where did it come from?" Pitcher said.

I shrugged. "I don't know." The only thing I could think of was that comment that Thea had made that day, about changing her will.

Joanne cracked a fortune cookie. "It is the question, not the answer," she said.

"Surely you don't believe in fortune cookies," Pitcher said.

"Yeah, I heard they were invented in San Francisco, not China," I said.

"And these were made in Brooklyn," she said. "So what?"

"What was it you wanted to discuss?" Pitcher said.

"I agree with Alex. Something doesn't seem right about this."

"You are concerned about the experiment," Pitcher said.

"I'm concerned for Alex," she said. "And for all of us. If this isn't legitimate…"

"I can take care of myself," I said.

She touched my hand, like she was saying, "I'm sure you think so." That honked me off a little. She's no smarter than me; better at math, more degrees. But not more brains. She'd already chewed me out earlier for giving the Stella twins my bank details. I thought, they're loaded, what would they steal from *me?* But I moved most of my money out to the savings account, anyway.

"That's a surrogate for something else, Dr. Marshall," Pitcher said.

"So you think this is all up-and-up?" she said.

"Perhaps not entirely, but our position should be clear. You are covering something else."

"I'm not—The whole imagery—the—what we're doing here; it's like trying to ram the Tower of Babel up the tunnel of light," she said.

"You make it sound like an act of violence," Pitcher said. "It is nothing of the kind."

"Says you," I said. There was a way in which Joanne had a point.

"It is nothing more than a few particles and negative matter," Pitcher said. "It is hardly a 'tower,' and hardly an invasion. Nimrod wished to invade heaven. I don't—I only want to see if it is there." He ate his cookie without bothering to look at the fortune.

I skipped the cookie—I always worry that I won't get a fortune. Superstitious, I know. But there it is.

So, after they gave Stu a deposit—when I knew they were serious—I told them the whole story. About wanting to know the exact day and time they were going to push the button; and about my other friend, the esteemed Professor Pitcher, and his little experiment. They seemed OK with everything; they set the date at three weeks later. At least, as far as I knew.

Imagine my surprise 10 days later when I arrived at the hospital to see Thea's bed empty. And then the cops waiting for me. Turned out that that document they'd shown me had been way out of date; superseded by another one Thea signed when she decided to undergo the experimental treatments. And there I was, the convict. With a 10 million dollar deposit in my account I couldn't explain.

Never mind that the Stella siblings each got 20 billion dollars that neither of them would have gotten if Thea had been able to change her will, like she'd told me she wanted to. We brought this up at trial; the DA demolished it, since no one would corroborate it.

And as for Stu? Yeah, he also had a 1 million dollar deposit in his account, too. They collared him also. But he fingered me; got 5 years, early release, and then a blog deal.

I was out on bail. My parole for my first conviction was over and the trial hadn't started yet. So I was out. And in between. In limbo, you could have said.

Anyway. Pitcher had me convinced that the lawyers he'd hired would get me out of this—they had gotten me bail, and so after that and what Thea had said, I'd had faith. Anyway, I'd really gotten into this Bible class, and not so much the stuff about death, like the sleeping with your ancestors, or when the class started talking about Joseph being turned into a mummy. I liked the stuff about the disasters. About Sodom and Gomorrah, or about Noah. Or about the tower of Babel. The kids in the class—all of them about 15 years younger than me—all thought it had to do with science. With "things we're not supposed to know." I thought it had to do with arrogance—that Nimrod—being a nimrod—wanted to bash down the heaven's door, not knock on it.

But really, I started thinking that maybe I deserved it. I kept going over and over it. I did get the Stella kids together with Stu the AS man. I knew—should have known—that Thea wouldn't have wanted it. Maybe I wasn't helping my own defense.

Now the thing I learned about expensive lawyers is; that, often, the most expensive ones win. So just because Pitcher got the University to hire really good lawyers, the Stella kids—with the money they stole when they killed their mother—hired better ones. Now, sure, the District Attorney was technically trying my case. But they hired a whole damn team to do the case for him. She just sat there and turned it all over to them. (When she ran for re-election—using me as her poster boy—she even claimed that the Stellas had saved the city money!)

During the trial, my lawyer tried to cross-examine the Stella twins, but that didn't work out too well. He tried to pin them on the money in my account and they claimed they gave me wire-transfer access, and I took the money. And the way the money was moved, he couldn't disprove it. And then he didn't want to let me testify, because he thought the other lawyer would cause more problems cross-examining me. I thought, maybe so, but that I could hold my own enough to create doubt. But I didn't, and the Stellas were great actors. Probably they knew exactly what to say, since Thea had been a lawyer herself. So when we tried to make a deal; even for life in prison, the DA wasn't interested.

At trial, Pitcher tried to defend me. He wrote a few blogs for the press, and even testified. In court, he told about how we really, really only wanted someone who really wanted to die; that we'd both be horrified at the idea of *murdering* someone for this. He gave an interview:

"Nearly everyone has heard the stories of near-death experiences. The tunnel, the light, etcetera. Now we have learned that this experience could be what you would expect to see if you were to somehow move from one universe to another. There would, in fact, be a wormhole. And the approach to the other side of the wormhole would appear bright, in contrast with the darkness of the hole itself. And the experimental verifications of string theory and dark matter and dark energy are indicating that those effects are caused by a neighboring universe interacting weakly with ours. So one hypothesis that might explain all of these facts would be that the consciousness of the dying person moves to that weakly interacting universe. This would be entirely speculative; but experimental verification is possible—I have the material and machinery ready. And who among us— perhaps those of us of weak faith in any case—would not want to know if there was someplace else after?"

Pitcher came to see me in my cell, after my last appeal. Not that he didn't come to see me otherwise. But that this time was different. He asked me, if I had to be executed, if it would be OK with me for me to be the way he got his experiment done.

"What the hell do I care?" I said.

I still wasn't thrilled with the idea of being executed. I'd thought, maybe I'd try to make a run for it; let them shoot me trying to escape instead of going gentle into that bad night. Better to go down resisting than being complicit in your own death. Not that I thought Pitcher would be able to get this accomplished anyway, and I said as much.

"I've got some favors I can call in," he said. "One aspect of reliance on the public sector for research funding; I have had to develop as many political contacts as any other lobbyist."

"And you couldn't use any of those to get me off?" I said.

"I did try, Alex," He said. "I kept running into the same problem. The one we had at trial, too. The Stellas and their money."

So, that's how we got here. In a lab three stories under Upper Manhattan, on a gurney, with a pair of IVs hooked up to a bunch of poisons. Oh. And an anesthetic.

The Warden, on hand to run the execution, gave a signal to the technician.

I heard Pitcher's machinery power up—a bunch of lasers were crossing over my head. They pushed the button.

Everything didn't go black. It went yellow. And black. The world dissolved into a black and yellow lines like the belly of a bee, and then it all went yellow—no more black.

The yellow cleared, and I could see again, and I was looking down on myself, with Pitcher running around behind his research assistants, running the machinery. And the execution doc running a scanner over me, ready to pronounce me dead.

Behind me, I felt something open. There was the tunnel. And the light. I suppose, by this point, I would have been one of the less-worried executionees; since I hadn't actually murdered anyone. I turned toward the light. And felt something rush past me, back down toward the lab. Something... *angry.*

I "turned around" to "see where" it had gone, and I could see, in the lab, pandemonium. Machinery was going dead. The Warden, executioners, witnesses from the media, the Stella siblings—all were desperately fiddling with their Pads and phones.

Pitcher looked ashen. Possibly worse than I did, and I was *dead*. He looked around, seemed to see that no one was paying attention to my body anymore. He grabbed something from a cabinet from under one of the desks, and ran to my side.

Then everything went black.

I woke up gasping. My chest hurt. My head hurt.

Pitcher was leaning over me. "Alex? Alex?"

"What the hell?" I said.

Pitcher held up one handle of a portable defibrillator in one hand, and a hypodermic with the other. "Just in case there might be a chance," he said, "I had these. This," he indicated the needle, "counteracts the effects of the chemicals."

"Great," I croaked. "Thanks." I tried to sit up, barely made it. I think I said already, my chest hurt.

The pandemonium I'd thought I'd seen was still breaking out. The prison staff had all left, the media were still trying to get their phones to work. The Stella siblings, and the lab assistants, all looked positively freaked.

"I guess your experiment didn't go very well?" I asked.

"I think I may have made a gigantic error," Pitcher said.

"Why? What's going on?"

"I think something came out when you were going in," he said.

"I thought I felt something," I said. "Something whizzing by me. Had never heard of that happening before."

"It ran through the connection from the particle probe into the computers and crashed them. And then the entire lab network. And then all the servers and computers in the building. We've heard from people upstairs and next door. Because we can't get in touch with anybody else. People have looked out the windows upstairs, and outside it's bedlam." He paused. "I have reason to believe that it is crashing the entire global communications system."

"That's nuts," I said. And then the lights went out.

We had emergency lights and flashlights, and they still worked. For a while. But nothing else ever did.